THEN, I FOUND YOU.

Contents

Copyright

Acknowledgements:

I wish to express my gratitude to all of the wonderful people who believed in me and that I was capable of telling stories to the world.

Especially to the editors/writers at Creative Book writers, you all rock.

Dedications:

"I love you as certain dark things are to be loved, in secret, between the shadow and the soul."

— Pablo Neruda, 100 Love Sonnets

To my husband, without whom, my achievements would never have been possible.

I love you for being so patient with me when I am lost in my imaginary world, consumed by the words.

Chapter One:

I was a little naïve in my younger days, in just about every department of life but especially sexually. But as time slips by, you find your way of dealing with it, and you learn to please and find the right amount of pleasure. In the beginning, I didn't know how to let men down gently without being rude. It never mattered how it all began; the end result was almost always the same; most of them were not as nice after getting in your undies. My heart had broken and rearranged many times, and my opinion of the other gender had morphed completely until I met Nick in my local bar.

He had just split up with his wife for having an affair with another woman while they had still been married. He stood out in the crowd when I spotted him, women swooning over him. He was very good looking with dark curly hair, dark features, and designer stubble; he was pure lust. I couldn't believe my luck that he was mates with Christof. Christof was one of my work colleagues in the sales office, as I was working on the export side of sales. Christof was French, and he dealt with the day to day relations of the French market with other European countries as he spoke many European languages.

You always imagine French guys as some hotties with that sexy accent along with the looks, but not Christof - he was back of the queue when he came into view. He had an average mousey cut, was short, with a stocky build and a sharp temper. He had a chip on his shoulder known as little man syndrome. He was always trying to get my attention, saying things like I was gorgeous and asking me why I wasn't dating. But as far I was concerned, it was only some banter, as he knew the type of guys I liked.

This was my opportunity to find out more about his mate as I headed towards the bar.

‘Hannah, ten o’clock at the bar with Christof,’ I whispered to my friend. ‘Hush, don’t make it too obvious,’ I added as I kept walking towards them.

The bar was getting busier as the music picked up the tempo.

‘Mmm, not bad, are you going to see what the score is with him?’ Hannah said, acknowledging that I had seen him first. That’s how we played it with the guys; whoever saw the guy first got the go-ahead.

‘Come on, then give me some moral support. I don’t want to be dealing with Christof if I am going to get this guy into bed tonight. We pushed our way through to where Christof and his mate stood waiting to be served at the bar.

‘Hi Christof, what are you doing here? I didn’t think you like coming out on a weekday.’ I smiled, standing close to his mate.

'Oh, hello, Liz, Hannah, what a pleasant surprise,' muttered Christof as he was about to be served. 'Would you two young ladies like a drink?' he asked us out of courtesy.

'Oh, yes, a beer, please,' I grinned.

'And I'll have the same please,' said Hannah mirroring my grin.

'So, aren't you going to introduce your friend to us?' I raised my eyebrow as I spoke to Christof, fishing for information.

'Oh yes, sorry this is Nick, he's staying with me for a while,' was all that Christof said, not giving much away. We went through all the pleasantries, but I wanted to know more about him. His dark features were drawing me in, especially his long dark hair and his "come to bed eyes." My mouth watered as I checked him out, hoping it didn't show. Nick was also looking me in the eye, knowing full well what I was after. He smiled mysteriously and started to chat about my experience working with Christof. Hannah kept Christof busy with her chit chat, leaving me with Nick. I stared at his strong shoulders hungrily and could feel any sense that was left in my body, flying out the window. Boy, I needed to fuck him. I clenched my thighs as the tension between us changed the conversation to sexual comments. I eventually found out that he was separated from his wife and was staying with Christof for a while until he could sort out a place of his own.

I was slightly nervous, having limited experience in the bedroom department. All the sex that I have ever had included a grope with guys where ever and the occasional blow job, but it was mainly in the back seat of their car. I was always up for a fuck in the back seat, not knowing when I was going to get it next, so wherever I could get it, I was game!

We had a couple more drinks before Nick asked if I wanted to leave. Hannah was in deep conversation with Christof, having a debate about animal rights, which was one of the topics she was so passionate about. Hannah was okay with us leaving, and so was Christof as the conversation started to heat up. We headed out to find a taxi back to Christof's flat.

We were in luck finding a taxi while waiting for a fare; we quickly jumped in, instructing the driver where to go. We headed back to Christof's flat, which was on the other side of the city. Nick's hands started to wander as soon as the ride started. He slipped them underneath my top; his strong hands cupped my breasts, squeezing them gently; I found this refreshing having as guys usually only groped me. I was getting aroused as he kissed my lips softly; this was an experience I had never had. The kind of action I usually had was hard and forced with a quick leg over. Nick paid the driver as we got out of the taxi and headed for the flat. I felt his closeness next to my body as we walked, with heat radiating from each other. We were straight into the bedroom as he slipped off my top, exposing my black lacy bra. He kissed me gently down my neck as his experienced fingers unhooked my bra from the back, dropping it to the floor.

My breasts looked perky; he took one of my hard nipples in his mouth and sucked gently. I started to moan with pleasure as I felt the sensations running through me like fire and ice mixed together. His skillful tongue flicked my nipple, making me wet and leading me to the verge of going crazy. For the first time in my life, I was with someone who knew how to please a woman.

God, I needed him inside me - I was bursting with need. I wound his hair around my fingers, pulling tightly as the sensation became stronger. I was panting heavily; 'Nick, I need you inside me,' I begged, breathing heavily as I whispered in his ear. He pushed me onto the bed, sliding off my jeans and undies, now having me totally naked and waiting for him to get inside me.

He also undressed quickly, exposing his manhood. His fit body was covered with hidden tattoos running all over, making him so sexy, dark, and mysterious. I opened my legs, waiting for him to enter me, but he pushed my legs further apart, lifting me slightly, taking his mouth to my wetness. His tongue danced around my clitoris, making small circles. All my senses kicked in as I moved my hips with his tongue, I was overwhelmed and on the verge of exploding as no one had done this to me before.

He slipped two fingers inside as he continued to cause magic with his tongue. My moans were loud enough to bring the walls down as I panted. Then I shuddered and had the best orgasm of my life. My breathing became shallow. Before I knew it, he slid inside me, pushing slowly as I could feel his full length filling me up. He held it inside me while he kissed me on the lips, making me taste my wetness. This experience was something else; everything was new. Usually, it was always the guy either wanting a blow job or hard sex. I was starting to learn something new, and I was enjoying it. He couldn't wait any longer as he picked up the pace, racing at full speed until we both came together. It was pure bliss and seduction.

I lay on the bed all worked up with sweat of an unexpected experience of sex and pleasure with a married man. It was so good - I needed more of this man's body and his sexual expertise.

'So how long have you been staying with Christof?' I asked casually, even though I was fishing to find his intentions of moving out.

'I've only been here a couple of days,' said Nick sounding as though he wasn't concerned about being separated from his wife.

‘Well, do you think you will get back with your ex?’ I asked, crossing my fingers, wishing that he would say no.

‘No, she’s had enough of me; she doesn’t trust me anymore,’ said Nick sounding casual and laughing at the end.

‘Oops, you did it more than once?’ I asked in surprise.

‘Well yes and no, the first time it was a mistake and second I was drunk,’ said Nick shrugging it off.

‘Oh, right,’ I said, lost for words. If I was going to try and keep him, I needed to please him. Guys usually like a good blow job, so if I treated him with as many blow jobs as possible, he might stay with me. As I said, I was naïve.

Nick laid there with his eyes closed, his dark features, tattoos, and delicious body making him the definition of the phrase ‘sex on legs.’

I ran my hand over his muscular chest, but he flinched slightly; at least he wasn't asleep. I leaned over and started to kiss his chest, making my way down to his length, which had started to grow for me to take in my mouth. He began to moan as I kissed his length, finding my way to the tip as a small drop leaked from his it, which I licked off. I took his length in my mouth. He was soon ready as I massaged his length with my tongue and eventually squeezed my hand over his balls. His moans grew louder, and his hand was resting on my head. I went for it, sucking hard, giving him the pleasure of coming in my mouth as I swallowed all his hot, salty liquid in one go, licking him dry.

'Fucking hell Liz, you do a good blow job.' moaned Nick as he fell back after coming in my mouth. I didn't say anything; I wanted him to ask me out so he could have this pleasure again; he could have as many blow jobs as he wanted.

I heard a key, and then the flat door open. Christof must be home, but as I looked at the time, it was past midnight. I would have to leave as I had work, the following day.

‘I’ll have to go,’ I said, seeing if Nick would ask me out. I jumped up from the bed as Nick grabbed me by the wrist, wrestling me onto the bed, smothering me with kisses. I squealed in delight as I must be having some effect on him.

‘Stay with me, will you, Liz?’ he whispered as he looked into my eyes; how could I resist? I needed to fuck him, all night if possible. ‘I’ll drop you off early tomorrow morning before I go to work.’

I grinned, looking into those deep eyes, saying, ‘We’re going to have sex all night; bring it on.’ I licked my lips, anticipating the next course.

Nick rolled me over onto my back, taking my breasts and giving them a gentle massage. He continued nipping my nipples with his teeth as he set his body between my legs.

'You've got nice breasts, just the right size and so perky,' Nick said as he gave them a little squeeze. I didn't say anything as I was moaning and enjoying the massage. His mouth made its way up to my neck, having it well exposed as I leaned as far back as I could with enjoyment. His mouth feasted on my exposed neck as he started to suck me in following my neck down into my cleavage. He was soon hard to enter me. My wetness showed my horniness, too, as he started sliding in hard. He used me like a piston running flat out and did not wait for me to come with him, but I was happy I was with him having sex and hoping for a lot more.

I let him rest for half an hour before straddling him, having my back to him with my butt in the air as I was bent down. I was kissing his body to his length, licking and kissing the sensitive areas of his length. I was sucking him hard to make him come, while his fingers were inside me, as he continued sucking on my butt. He had got to ask me out, considering what I had been doing to him. Throughout the night, we had sex as much as he could take, and I kept making sure I was keeping him happy so he would ask me out. The only thing on my mind was, was he going to ask me out?

We only had a couple of hours of sleep before it was time to go. Nick had a shower while I dressed as I would have one when I got back to my flat, as I would have to change for work. Nick looked hot in his grey suit and designer stubble; he was practically sex on legs.

When he pulled up outside my flat, it was just after 7 am which gave me plenty of time for a shower and a change of clothes as I was allowed flexible hours.

‘Well,’ I said, not wanting to get out of the car, ‘I enjoyed last night. Thank you.’ I grinned at him.

‘So did I,’ replied Nick grinning back. ‘Would you like a rerun, Liz?’ asked Nick, smirking knowing I would. How could I resist the sex god sitting next to me?

‘When were you thinking?’ I asked, dancing inside with joy.

‘Thursday next week. Is that okay with you?’ said Nick.

‘Err yeah, okay,’ I said, thinking it would have been either Friday or Saturday evening. It was decided then that he would come to pick me up at 7 pm the following Thursday. I gave him a quick kiss and jumped out of his car, but before I could turn around to wave, he had gone, leaving me on the pavement as though he had someone to see. Oh well, I suppose Thursday was better than nothing at all, but it would have been nice having a weekend with him.

I was in for work at 8.30 am; Christof was already in with the phone to his ear, not seeing me come in. I needed a coffee to wake me up having only a couple of hours of sleep, but that was worth it. While I was in the staff kitchen, making a coffee, Christof came in with his empty mug.

'Makes me one too, would you please, Liz?' He requested dumping his mug next to mine.

'What? Did your last slave die-off jesting to Christof?' I teased.

'Liz, I don't want to sound too blunt, but just be careful of Nick, I don't want you to get hurt. I don't know what he has told you, but he's on the rebound and doesn't know what he wants,' said Christof sounding concerned for me.

'Of course, Christof, you would say that and put the dampeners on it,' I said, sounding miffed. He picked up his coffee as I poured hot water into his mug, and he disappeared out of the staff kitchen, but not before he could say, 'Oh, and by the way, I could hear you two all-night,' while smirking as he closed the door.

The following night I met up with Hannah, and we decided to go to the local night club. I still was thinking of Nick and the night with him. It was an experience I had never shared with anyone else, and I wanted more. It was nearly eleven pm by the time we arrived at the night club. It was heaving being a Friday night, and we had to push our way through to the bar. We both were reasonably merry as we had a few drinks before coming in as the night club drinks were more expensive. On the odd occasion that guys would buy us a drink, they always expected something back in return. We purchased our first drinks and started to scan the night club for any potential guys noticing a group of ten guys looking like a stag night as one of the guys had a ball and chain around his neck.

Hannah had seen them as we moved in on them to find the best guys out of the bunch. Of course, they had to be drunk with the exception of one guy as he was driving the minibus. Hannah took a shine to him straight away as a conversation got underway. I pulled my top down at the hem, making my cleavage show a little more before walking ahead, pretending to bump into them on purpose just to start a conversation. An arm grappled me around the waist as a tall guy with short hair gave me a sloppy kiss on the cheek. I laughed it off, as he tried to kiss me on the lips, this time, his kiss was hard and wet with a taste of whiskey which he was drinking. I nearly gagged; I hated the taste of whiskey, I tried to pulling away, but he squeezed me tighter. The guy had bear-hugged me, and I figured that I needed help.

Fuck, where was Hannah when I needed her? I could just see her talking to the sober guy. I wrestled with the guy hugging me as we fell onto the floor, his grip was released by the fall, and I escaped, pulling myself together after the embarrassment.

It was like being back to the normal guys groping. I had had enough as my thoughts turned to Nick and having to wait a week before I was with him again. Hannah came over,

'Liz, are you okay?' she asked, touching my arm.

'Yeah, it's just the same old things all over again, blokes being total jerks,' I said, slightly pissed off. The guy who Hannah was talking with was waiting for her to return, so I asked her if it was okay with her if I went home, and she stayed with the guy she was talking to.

'Are you sure you're alright, Liz?' asked Hannah, slightly concerned now.

'No, you stay, don't worry about me,' I assured her, hugging her before I disappeared from the night club. Why did things suddenly feel different all of a sudden? I kept thinking as I decided to walk home instead of getting a taxi. It was like going back to eating dry grass after getting a taste of steak. I needed more steak; I needed Nick.

I rang Hannah the following morning to see if she was going out later that evening.

'Um, sorry, Liz, Paul's asked me out tonight, and I said yes I would see him tonight,' said Hannah sounding sheepish.

'Oh, okay, I take it went well then?' I asked, sounding a little miffed.

'Mmm yeah, he's quite nice,' said Hannah sounding slightly upbeat.

'Nice. I'll give you a ring in the week then.' I said my goodbyes before pressing the off button on my phone.

O bollocks! What the fuck am I going to do now that my other friends have partners, including my two flatmates? The thought somehow pushed me into depression.

It seemed a long week before Nick came to pick me up on Thursday, finally. I wasn't sure what to wear, I didn't know where he was taking me, so I slipped on a short dress and heels. It was soon seven pm, and Nick hadn't turned up. Had he changed his mind? I thought pacing the living room, glancing out of the flat window. I was in the flat on my own, which I had been since I had left Hannah the Saturday night with Paul. All week I had been thinking about this night with Nick, having been alone either watching TV or listening to music all week in the evenings. Lottie and Emma seemed to be spending more time with their fuck buddies, too, which was more than what I was getting. Nick still hadn't turned up by seven-thirty pm. I had given up; my excitement was gone, pushing me to feel more depressed. I slowly dragged myself back my bedroom to change in something more comfortable to lounge out in as the doorbell rang. I opened the door to find Nick looking harassed.

'Sorry, Liz, my wife turned up as I was going out said.' Nick was apologizing but did not explain what his wife wanted. I didn't push it. I just needed his naked body on mine.

'So, where are we going?' I asked now that he had turned up at last.

'Back to the flat if you want, or we could stay in?' said Nick, smirking.

'Err well, I share with two flatmates, and it gets a bit crowded in here sometimes.' I made an excuse knowing that my bedroom was a total mess, plus I only had a single bed.

‘Sure, okay then back to mine then,’ muttered Nick as he turned around, heading back to the car. He looked hot as ever. It didn’t matter what he wore. He was sex on legs always, even better in the buff with him on top of me giving me oral first and then hard sex.

As Nick set off back to Christof’s flat, I approached the subject of asking him what had he been doing all week trying to sound as casual as I could.

‘I had a few late nights at work catching up on some sleep and went out with a few mates at the weekend,’ said Nick sounding normal.

‘So you didn’t see your wife then?’ I asked out of curiosity.

‘Well, she was out with her mates over the weekend, and I caught up with her then,’ said Nick. I was about to ask him something else when we arrived at the flat. Christof was out, which I found a little unusual, not being a person to go out in the evening's mid-week.

'Where's Christof tonight?' I knew I sounded nosy but asked anyway,

'He was out with us on the weekend, and he took a fancy for one of my wife's friends, Sasha, so he's seeing her tonight.' Nick filled me in, smiling.

'Oh, he's a sly one, I'll have to ask him about his date,' I said grinning.

We walked into the kitchen, where Nick switched the kettle on.

'Would you like some coffee?' Nick asked while grabbing a couple of clean mugs.

'Yes, please.' I wrapped my arms around his waist, pressing my breasts on his back as I hugged him tightly.

'If you keep going, you will have to have it right here,' said Nick moaning slightly as I slid my hand down to the inside of his trousers. He was already aroused, ready for action. I started to unbutton his trousers, pulling his zip down, taking his length in my hand as I stood from the back of him, pressing my breasts harder into his back. He spun around, facing me as my hands let go of his length. I knelt down to take him in my mouth as I sucked him hard, knowing he would come straight away, his hand leaning on the kitchen countertop while the other on top of my head moving with the rhythm of my mouth on his length, moaning in the pleasure I was giving him. Within seconds he had come, and I swallowed his hot salty liquid licking his length dry before standing and kissing him gently on the lips.

'Oh god, Liz, that was good,' said Nick sounding satisfied. I was pleased with my actions, knowing I had pleased him and well aware that a lot of wild action was in store for us that night.

Chapter Two:

Nick finished making the coffee and brought the mugs into his bedroom as we sat on the bed. He switched on the TV, asking if I wanted to watch anything in particular.

"No, but I can think of something else to do." I licked my lips and smirked at him.

"Liz, you will bloody kill me if you keep blowing me like that," said Nick, grinning at me. I moved over to straddle him as my dress slid up to my waist. I slipped the dress over my head to expose my black lacy bra and undies and bent forward slightly, revealing a glimpse of my cleavage, hoping he would make the next move. Nick stared at my cleavage as he unhooked my bra, releasing my breasts. He kissed them as his hands squeezed them together.

He rolled my nipples between his thumb and index finger, urging me to throw my head back in pleasure as the sensation kicked in. My wetness was starting to drip, anticipating for him to go down on me. He pushed me on my back, sliding my undies as he nudged my legs apart to go down on me. I was in ecstasy, his tongue playing with my clit with his fingers inside me, hitting the right spot. My multiple orgasms exploded around his skilled tongue and fingers playing with me.

He started to drink in my wetness before coming up and kissing me hard on the lips, making me taste my wetness again. I enjoyed this moment and secretly hoped to have many more like these. I was panting with the force of my orgasm as I whispered in his ear, asking if he was ready for my mouth as I started to strip him off as though I was unwrapping a Christmas present to find a surprise.

I had him stretched out on the bed naked ready for me to pleasure him. I started kissing him slowly from the mouth to his hardened nipples, he moaned with his head resting back, and his eye closed as I made my way down slowly to his length. He was waiting for me to put him into my mouth, but first I took hold of his balls gently caressing and kissing them, while he moaned my name. I felt good, powerful because I was making him felt like this, and I had that effect over him; I needed him to stay with me.

I slowly licked his length, flicking my tongue on his tip as a tear appeared, he was ready to explode in my mouth, and I made him wait, teasing his length.

"Liz, you're fucking killing me," he moaned and begged simultaneously as he grew increasingly impatient. He took hold of my head with his hand, pushing me down to suck him harder till he was at the brink of coming. I obliged, sucking him harder, and within seconds he had come; I caught all his hot salty liquid in my mouth and swallowed, licking him completely dry.

"Liz, you are a fucking tease, you're bloody going to kill me," said Nick once again, panting and beads of sweat showing on his cheeks.

After a few minutes, we heard Christof coming in after his evening out at his date. *I will ask him in the morning about that*, I thought as I lay in Nick's arms, taking a breather from our workout in the bed.

"I'll soon have to be going," I said, trying not to overstay my welcome.

"It's ok, Liz; I'll drop you off at 7 am when I go to work." Nick murmured in my ear.

"Mm, I like the sound of that," I replied, kissing him on the lips as I straddled him to make the most of the time we had until the morning.

I was sucking him most of the night hoping he would be asking me to see him again, even if it was only one night in the week, I was in utopia. Little did I know about what I was getting myself into?

I came home at 7 am with Nick with a promise that he would see me again the following Thursday; it was better than nothing as he drove off with no care in the world. Christof was already at work when I got in, so I went to make a coffee in the staff kitchen. I was about to walk out with my coffee as Christof came in. He was looking like a cat that had gotten the cream.

"Whoa, you're looking happy for a change," I said before I went on to say, "Good night, then?" I wondered if he would say anything about his date.

"Well, you certainly had one, Liz. I heard you two screaming at god knows what time," said Christof smirking and raising his brows at me. I decided to stay quiet as I did not know anything about his date yet, so he didn't need to know about mine. I went back to the office and noticed a new face amongst us.

"Hmm, I wonder where this one has come from?" I thought to myself, looking at the tall fit guy talking to my boss Jon.

Jon was going around to all the staff in the office to introduce him to everyone. I waited for my turn, wanting to know more about this fit guy. Nick was lush, but only seeing him once a week meant I needed more; unless he was married; then, I didn't want the baggage to go with it. I had just finished my call when Jon came around with the guy in question. I looked him up and down; yep, he was a candidate if he was single.

"Liz this is Dave he has come up from our head office and is in charge of fitting teams on the site for our clients," said Jon taking a side step for Dave to shake hands with me, but did he rub his fingers into my palm before pulling back with a smirk?

"So, he's a quick worker." I thought, smiling back, waiting for him to speak, but Jon had moved on to introduce him to Christof. Fuck, I'll have to find out more about him later as gossip went around the office quickly, especially if it's juicy.

I was finding it extremely hard being stuck at home on the weekend, having no one to go out with. Everyone I knew had a partner; lucky them. Alan and Lee had come around to stay the night, having to hear them through the walls made me envious, hearing their moans and squeals of enjoyment; it was making me wet, so I had to turn up the volume on the TV. I had had enough and finally decided to go out to a night club on my own.

Like I said earlier, with only seeing Nick once a week, I needed more. Also, as the weeks went by, he seemed to have changed, but I didn't push it, I didn't want to lose what I had on the Thursday evenings with him.

It was nearly 10 pm before I left home and headed to the nearest night club, dressed in a simple black short dress with black heels and a light coating of make-up. By the time I arrived, it was gone 10.45 with the night club heaving with clubbers and the music playing loud. Just as well being on my own as if I was with someone, they wouldn't be able to hear me speak. I pushed my way through to the bar with the odd guy ogling me and passing strange sexual comments, but my mind was on Nick knowing somehow, he was going to let me down, and it was going to kill me.

I decided I would have a gin and tonic taking it to the upstairs balcony to view the area of the clubbers and the dance floor. There were a few people I knew from our college days with one or two new faces, but there weren't any guys that stood out in the crowd. Not only that, but half were drunk wearing beer goggles groping women who weren't particularly appealing, being drunk themselves and loud. A couple of guys came up to me, one of them swaying, making a big arse of himself as his mate tried to chat with me. He put his arm over my shoulder, and I realized that he wasn't as bad as his mate. His hand started to wander to my breast, giving a squeeze to test my reaction. I asked myself, was I feeling this, and did I need him inside me? I thought I would play him and see how far he would go, that too if he could make it.

The balcony was slightly quieter as I whispered in his ear. "You want sex?" I asked it to test him out. There was a surprised look on his face.

"Why, you are up for it?"

"Yeah, where are we going?" I asked; it was his call.

"I'll have to get the keys off my mate; we'll use his car," he said, holding onto my wrist as we walked down to the main dance floor area to find his mate. His other mate was flat out asleep on the seating area upstairs. We found the guy, and he handed his keys over. We made our way to the car parking at the back of the night club. It had a large back seat; I slid across. The guy seemed to have sobered up a little as he started running his hand up my dress slipping them in my undies. He kissed my neck, and suddenly, thoughts of Nick crept over me. I needed this. I could feel his hand on my breast, squeezing hard.

Despite the harshness I was aroused; wanting it badly, I unzipped his trousers and positioned myself for him to enter me. I took off my undies in readiness for his entry. He was pulling my dress off my shoulder, trying to gain access to more of my cleavage. I stopped him; you'll have to unzip me, I said, leaning forward as he did, slipping the dress off my shoulders to reveal my plain black bra. He unhooked it, releasing my breasts; His eyes feasted on my breasts as he massaged and squeezed them with excitement. I let him have his moment of enjoyment with my breasts. I was wet, but not by him; it was just the need, I needed him inside. After a couple of minutes of groping my breasts, I held his length coaxing it to enter me. I lifted my dress, exposing my entrance for him to enter, and to my utter surprise, he went down on me, pulling me flat onto the back seat of the car, sucking my wetness.

I moaned with the pleasure of surprise as he made me come, too quick. His hand still squeezing my breast as his tongue played with my clit. By the time he came up, I had come twice. He came up fast and entered me hard, pumping me like a piston until he came. We lay there a few minutes before he moved.

"God, I needed that," he said, sounding relieved.

"Oh, I'm a relief?" I said with sarcasm.

"Sorry, I didn't mean it like that. It's just that my wife is off sex, and I needed a release," he said, sounding serious and sober.

"I'll tell you what? It's your lucky night; you can play with my body and keep making me come if you want." I told him in an inviting tone. I didn't have to repeat myself as he jumped straight in squeezing and pulling at my breasts again, it was like releasing a child into a sweet shop to help themselves. My wetness was overflowing as he went down first, pumping me as his tongue played me, making me come over and over again. He had given me an hour of pleasuring until his hardness was ready to enter me.

"Fuck me hard so you can have your pleasure," I said, sweating and panting with all the orgasms hitting me one after another. Once he had exhausted all angles, he was knackered. I wasn't going to blow him; I wanted my pleasure.

We pulled ourselves together and got dressed. He asked to see me again, but I declined by saying that I didn't want baggage.

"I thought I'd ask; you are pretty, and you have a lovely sexy body any man would die for," he said in a sincere tone.

"Oh, thanks," was all I said, not taking the compliment seriously. I was always bad with compliments, not knowing whether they was true or not. We kissed goodbyes as he went back into the night club while I walked home happier than I was a few hours ago.

Joanne had found some gossip on Dave from work. He was married with a couple of young kids; she had seen them in the supermarket when she had stopped for a quick chat. Dave did a lot of travelling around the country to organize teams of fitters to build the modules on the client's site but has come back into the office to overseeing a large project for a client, which is worth a lot of money.

"Julie told me that he had been trying to chat her up the same day he arrived and asked her out," said Joanne disapprovingly.

"Well, I don't know. He probably doesn't get it at home," I said, thinking about the guy I had sex within the back of the car over the weekend.

"Yeah, you're probably right there, Liz," said Joanne getting up to for lunch.

Thursday evening had soon come around, my evening with Nick, but he wasn't showing the enthusiasm of seeing me as he had done a few weeks ago despite pulling all the stunts out to please him to the limit. I was falling in love with him, with him pleasuring me and thinking we had something special.

Nick was late again, as it was after 8 pm. I knew something was wrong as he stood on the doorstep, looking deep in thought as though he was worried about something. It didn't matter what he wore; he always looked like sex on legs. I had just changed my clothes, thinking he was going to let me down. I had slipped my silk robe over me when I opened the door.

"Sorry, I'm late," said Nick stepping inside and closing the door behind him. I made nothing of it, walking into the living room.

"Lottie and Emma are out tonight, so I'm on my own; I was listing to music in my bedroom," I told him as the music played through into the living room. Nick stood behind me, wrapping his arms around my waist to untie my robe. It was made of silk and it slipped off easily. His experienced hands cupped my breasts as I held my head back moaning, feeling aroused by his touch.

"I've missed this," I whispered, moaning in pleasure as he kissed my neck, turning me around, making his way down my body.

"God, I've waited so long for this evening to come," he said as he pushed me on the sofa, spreading my legs to take my wetness.

"I love you so much, Nick," I whispered, not realizing what I had said. He continued playing with my wetness with his tongue as he inserted his fingers inside me, hitting my sensitive spot, making me come at once. Our mouths met tasting my wetness as I started to undo his trousers to give his length much needed attention. I pushed him back to wrap my mouth over his length sucking hard to relieve him within seconds drinking all his liquid,

"Nick, do you want to go to my bedroom?" I asked, knowing my room was tidy.

"Liz, I need to say something," said Nick, suddenly looking uncomfortable. I sat up, looking worried about what he was going to say.

"Liz, you're a pretty girl, and I have never known anyone as good as you, giving a guy a blow job as you do. But the thing is, my wife wants me back, and I still love her," he dropped the bomb, rubbing his hand over his designer stubble. I knew something was wrong when he had halted at the door before. I felt I had just been hit in the stomach; I was gutted at the thought of not seeing him anymore; my eyes started to moisten as I asked him.

"Nick, would you stay with me just for tonight?"

"Liz, I have to go. I have moved out of the flat and have everything in my car to go home to my wife," said Nick getting up to leave.

"Nick, please," I begged, holding onto his arm, hoping he would change his mind.

"Sorry, Liz, it's been good, but I have to go." he made his way to the door now; he had his pleasure from me. Tears started to drip from the corner of my eyes, thinking I will not see him again and have that pleasure with him. I was gutted.

"I am sorry, Liz, I have to go." Were his last words as he opened the door, leaving me standing as he drove off down the road? I closed the door, sliding down as I sobbed my heart out for losing Nick to his wife. The playlist was still playing as the song 'Alone' by Heart started to play, bringing my sobs back in buckets.

I was pleased that Christof wasn't working today. I wouldn't have been able to cope if he mentioned Nick moving out to go back to his wife. Now my Thursday dates with him had finished. Dave was on full form as banter started around the office, I managed a forced smile, trying to join it as my heart wasn't in it. I was glad 5 pm had come at last. I made a quick exit knowing that I would burst into tears at any time.

Lottie and Emma were in when I got home. Emma had just put a large pizza in the oven as I walked in.

“Hi Liz, we haven’t seen much of you lately, have we Lottie?” She hugged me.

“No, we need a catch-up, Liz,” said Lottie joining the hug. My lips started to wobble, eventually bursting into tears.

“Oh, Liz, what’s wrong?” asked Lottie as she came over to hug me again. Emma was soon out of the kitchen, too, after hearing my sobs.

“Come on, Liz, sit down and tell us what is the matter,” said Lottie sounding concerned. Lottie and Emma sat down, waiting for me to start.

“I have been so stupid getting involved with a married man, I was starting to fall in love with him, and he made me feel so good," I began, stuttering with my sobs kicking in between my sentences. Lottie and Emma both hugged me in silence until I had finished.

"Oh Liz, I'm so sorry, but I'm not sorry to say you will get over him," said Emma sounding practical.

"I know, but it hurts so much," I said as a sob came out again.

"It will take some time, Liz," added Lottie, sounding optimistic.

"Yeah, I suppose, you're both right." I sniffed. They had made me feel a lot better like I was not alone.

As the weeks and months went by, I soon toughened up with men by switching off and not getting attached unless they were single and had no baggage. I continued to go the night club mixing with the guys flirting and teasing them knowing what they wanted, but it was my call if I did or not. For the first couple of months, I had sex with guys every time I was at the night club to erase the feeling I had for Nick, which eventually faded away.

Christof didn't comment on Nick moving out, considering it would hurt me knowing I could be sensitive sometimes. Dave was still pushing as we bantered. As time went by, his project had nearly come to an end with having to go down to the client's site to organize the teams to build the modules. Dave kept on hounding me to come down to meet him at the hotel he was staying at, but after a couple of weeks, I gave in. This meant I had to drive, not having any experience in driving in bad weather, as winter had set in.

Also, I had to remind myself over and over again that it was for my good. Dave was no different from Nick, and my heart was not ready to go through another experience like that. I needed to find and settle on someone else, someone who suited me and was not just playing around like the rest of them.

Chapter Three:

It was Monday morning in mid-January; the weather had been cold with freezing temperatures and snow showers. I was supposed to go down to meet Dave at a hotel near where he was working. He was working on a job as in charge of a team of guys having to complete their task before the weekend. The weather was unpredictable, so I didn't risk it being a two-hour journey down the motorway. It would have been my first physical, sexual encounter with him. Engaging in a lot of banter and flirting in the office over the last six months was a whole lot different than shagging him for real.

I was in the staff kitchen, making coffee when Dave came in.

'Hey, what happened to you Friday night?' he asked, sounding rather pissed.

‘Erm well, the weather wasn’t too good, so I didn’t bother coming.’ I shrugged, not meeting his eyes.

‘I was waiting for you. I thought you said you were coming down and would stay over,’ said Dave sounding even more pissed off. I was pouring the boiling hot water into my mug as he turned around with his arms in the air and yelled, ‘You are nothing but a fucking cock teaser giving me the ‘Come on’ sign ever since I came up here! What is a man supposed to do when you are giving those signals?’ and with that, he was gone.

I was gobsmacked. I hadn’t been giving him the signal, well not intentionally at least. Yes, I was going down to meet him at the hotel but shied away because of the weather. I had never driven all that long and wasn’t confident driving in bad weather. It was not my fault his testosterone level was high waiting to be released on me. I knew that he was married, but deep down, I felt an urge to be chased with that control over the male species.

Dave had been chasing me since the day he came up from the head office. He was renowned for affairs, but I didn't have to lead him on, he did that himself, so I just went with it. I had been there a year, but after that outburst in what he had just said made me feel like a sex object and a cock teaser. The atmosphere at work when he came into the office wasn't the same; you could cut the atmosphere with a knife. It was time for me to look for another job. After all, it's never a good idea to get involved with colleagues in the workplace.

It took me three months to find another job in a similar role; in addition, I took a part-time job working behind a bar three nights a week. I shared a flat with two other girls, both of whom had partners, and it made me feel like a spare part in the evenings with them bonking in their bedrooms. Listening to the noise of their sexual exploits, I was missing sex; I needed sex.

All my friends had a partner apart from me. I was the only one having one-night stands; so, taking another job in the bar was the next best thing. At least you were being paid to socialize with the customers.

I had been working at the bar for two weeks when this guy came in with his mate. I had never seen him around before; also, his looks were distinguished with black curly hair, dark eyebrows, and dark eyes, making his features stand out. His build was average but muscular underneath, and he was dressed casually in jeans and a tee-shirt. The other guy with him was thick set with his tee-shirt tight across his stomach and was wearing slightly baggy jeans and a belt to keep them up.

He came across to the bar with his mate behind him; obviously, he was in charge. He asked for two pints of beer, and I smiled as I served them, but he made no conversation while serving them. I could see his mate watching me walking down to the till, and felt his eyes peeling my dress off. They stood at the bar chatting as I served more customers; they were mainly couples, with the older guys in tonight with it being a Thursday.

I was being watched by the fat guy with comments being passed to his mate with the dark curly hair.

'Mm, how can I start this conversation up?' I thought to myself, but his mate was butting in. I went along with it only to see if this mate would open up. But as the night went on, it was falling on deaf ears, as just before closing time, they both left. 'Fuck, I will have to up my game if I'm going to get laid with this gorgeous guy and not his mate,' I muttered to myself, hoping to see him again.

A couple of weeks later, they were back wearing the same clothes; I secretly hoped they had not worn them all this time. Fatty was full of himself giving me the signals, and though it was true that I wanted sex, I wasn't that desperate. Big boy had disappeared to the men's room, and I sighed in relief.

'He's a bit full-on, but he can't manage it,' said the curly-headed guy as his mate left. So this was my cue to up my game and went for it.

'Ahaan, I take it that you can,' I teased him, licking my lips and coming on to him.

'How about we try it out sometime?' he suggested.

'Hmm, I'll have to think about that,' I teased him licking my lips again, but before I could say anything, his mate had come back. I went off to serve customers, but by the time I had finished, I turned around and found that they had gone. Shit, I had missed him. I could have shagged him that night. My arousal after talking to him was making me wet below.

It was after 11.30 pm when I left the bar, heading off home. I heard someone calling me by my name. 'Who the hell is this voice coming from out of the shadows?' I looked around slightly creeped out. To my utter shock, it was the guy with the curly hair.

I couldn't believe my luck, he had been waiting for me, but where was his mate?

'Oh hello, what are you doing here at this time of night?' I asked.

'Waiting for you, I thought we would go back to my place and finish our conversation off before my mate came back,' said Curly.

'Wow, you don't hang about, do you? But what makes you think I'll come back with you,' I finished with a smirk.

'Because I know you're up for it,' said curly, now standing close with his hands on my shoulders looking into my eyes. Fucking hell, I was gagging for it. He was making me wet even with his touch, and then he kissed me, moving in closer and enveloping me in his arms as he sucked me in. Resistance was futile - I had to go and fuck him despite the fact I knew nothing about him.

He only lived two streets away from me, his flat was basic, a typical bachelor pad with no signs of a woman living with him. It was like the movie 'fatal attraction'; as he unlocked his door, we started ripping off each other's clothes heading straight for the bedroom. There was no foreplay with his hardness waiting to enter me and my wetness ready to receive him. We fucked hard, but he was too quick shooting his lot before I had a chance to come. Fuck, he was loaded. When was the last time he fucked? We lay on the bed, sweating, half-dressed and in silence. I didn't know anything about this guy, but I wanted to know more. After a couple of minutes, I asked him his name, 'Jo,' he said, giving nothing away.

'Don't you have a second name?' I asked.

'Henderson,' His replies were short, like his timings in sex.

'Ok, and what do you do?' I continued asking.

'I work on the rigs, so I'm away eight weeks and three weeks off.'

'So when do you go back?' I asked, thinking if I'd see him again soon.

'I've got just under a week left,' was all that he said. I had to ask him. I needed to see him again before he went back, but I thought I would leave it to see if he would say anything first. I didn't want to spoil the rest of the night, and to feel needy.

We laid there for about half an hour when he rolled over, taking hold of my breasts, squeezing them tight and pressing his lips hard onto my nipples, biting them slightly between his teeth. His was getting hard, pulling me down on the bed as he straddled over me. It felt good feeling his hardness on my body. He kissed me on my neck, sucking hard on my skin as he made his way down to my neat shaven bush. His hard kissing hurt in the tender places, making me wince in slight pain, but he didn't say anything. He moved up to me, entering his length hard inside, pushing so hard I felt as though his balls were in. I was just working up to come, but he got there before me shooting his lot flopping on top of me, looking exhausted. 'Fuck! Why he couldn't wait for me so we could come together?'

It was after 2.30 am, and I had work in the morning, but I didn't want to go. I could leave at 6 am and nip home for a quick shower and a change of clothes, but I just wanted to keep shagging this guy. I had some catching up to do not know when my next shag will be. He wasn't complaining; we were totally naked, exposing all our hidden secrets of intimate areas and tattoos. This guy was making my mouth water, so I went down, sucking his hard length; he was moaning, pushing my head with his hands going with the motions of his pleasure. He soon came, and I swallowed his hot salty liquid. He had a good sex drive, and we had wild sex until he fell asleep.

Morning came too soon. It was 6 am already, and even though I didn't want to go back, I had to. By now, I had lost count of how many times we had fucked. As I got out of the ruffled bed, I looked at Jo, fast asleep, which wasn't a surprise as he had performed well. I gathered my things and quickly slipped them on, making my way to the bathroom before leaving. I needed to see him again before he went back to the rigs, but I didn't want to wake him. So, I left quietly, closing the door behind me. I just hoped he would come and see me at the bar where I was working.

I just made it in time for work by two minutes, my mind cast back to my all-night of sex. My head was in the clouds. I was still thinking of last night and making myself wet again. Christ, my hormones were on a high; I had only sex on my brain. Seated at my desk, I switched on my computer and logged on to read my emails.

Needing coffee, I went to the staff kitchen to find Liam was already in and had just made a coffee for himself.

'Kettle's boiled,' he said as he looked up, staring at me.

'Ok, thanks,' I went on, not making eye contact as my brain was still in my undies.

'Looks like you have had a good night,' said Liam with a smirk as he stopped near the door staring at me.

'Why? What makes you think that?' I asked, sounding surprised by his tone.

'You have love bites on your neck, Liz,' he said with another smirk.

'Oh,' I shrugged it off and carried on making my coffee. Liam left, leaving me on my own to finish making my coffee. As I walked back from the staff kitchen, I was getting stared at, my colleagues smirking. Had I spilt something on me, or did I have a mark on my face or something?

Putting my coffee on my desk, I turned to Anne. 'Anne, why are people smirking? Am I missing something here?' I asked with a frown.

'Can't you see it, Liz? You need to look at yourself in the mirror,' said Anne. I went to the ladies' and stood in front of the mirror, horrified. I hadn't realized he had sucked me that hard leaving love bites all over my neck and down my front where I was exposed with my blouse down to my cleavage. Fuck what were people going to think of me? I hadn't checked myself this morning after having a quick shower and being in a rush, I had slipped on the nearest thing available in the wardrobe. Fuck, fuck, fuck, I had to keep a low profile in the office now, especially the managers being older and would frown upon my love bites.

I just hoped I wasn't asked to take anything into them. The day dragged on. I was clock-watching waiting to jump ship at 5 pm, and I had to work at the bar. I couldn't have these showing to the public.

It was 5.15 pm by the time I started to close my computer. I had been lucky not to bump into any management all day. I took my mug into the staff kitchen to wash it with my head down and avoiding eye contact as the staff left the building. Since it was Friday, some were heading home and some to the nearest bars to unwind the stresses of the day.

As I was washing my mug, I heard the door open as someone came in. I ignored them, not wanting them to see what I had been up to the previous night.

'Oh, I didn't think there would be anyone in here.' said a voice from behind.

‘I’ll be gone in a minute,’ I muttered, not turning around to see who it was.

‘You don’t have to go on my account.’ said the unknown voice. I finished drying my mug, putting it to one side. I turned around where stood a tall guy about ten years older than me with uncut messy blonde hair, piercing blue eyes, and a fit body standing close in front of me.

I was taken aback with the closeness, looking into his blue eyes as he smiled; I had never seen him before.

‘Oh, hello,’ I said, trying to avoid him seeing the marks on my neck as I stepped to one side to walk past him.

‘It’s nice to meet other staff members in the company as I don’t get out of the office much,’ said the stranger in front of me. I wanted to go for two reasons: one because of my love bites and secondly, I was working at the bar tonight. I had to somehow disguise the marks before starting my shift at the bar. I didn't want to be rude and ignore him, so I glanced up at him and said, 'Well, it's nice to meet you, but I'm sorry I have to be somewhere at 7 pm.'

'God, I bet he thinks I'll be getting laid again tonight,' I cursed myself.

'I better let you go then, Liz; by the way, my name is Gus. It's a pleasure to meet you.'

'Hmm, likewise,' and with that, I was out of the door, quickly collecting my coat and bag heading for the main entrance.

Emma and Lottie were in as I could hear the music blurring out. All three of us used to go out clubbing, and we always had guys hanging around us, probably because of Lottie's large breasts and mainly because she dressed to show their potential. It was a normal one-night stand where we all compared notes of the evening's sexual exploits and marked them one out of ten, and finally finding the ones they wanted to keep for a while until they needed a change.

None of us would bring anyone back to the flat; it was always at their place unless they wanted to see you again with a few dates before they would be allowed to the flat. I wasn't that lucky. We all had been living together for nearly two years.

Before coming here, I had been looking to rent a flat on my own but had to share due to the salary I was on. I couldn't afford to rent on my own yet, so seeing an advertisement in the café about Emma and Lottie looking for a third person to share as the previous flatmate had moved into her boyfriend's flat. I was lucky due to the fact that they had just put the advert in the shop window and I was the first to apply. We got on like a house on fire, having the same sense of humor and eventually sexual exploits. Emma managed to persuade me into having a couple of tattoos on the inner top sides of legs, with only those who sexually aroused me would see them. I had to be inebriated to have them done being in a tender area, not feeling the pain as much with the needles pummeling my skin soaking in the colours. It was a couple of weeks before I was back in the saddle experiencing sexual comments on my tats.

Emma worked in the design and art industry and was tall with a slender frame with short spikey hair which varied in colour depending on the mood she was in at the time, today her hair was red with pink highlights it suited her. She also had body piercings in her tongue and nose, with one just added recently to her clitoris. Her fuck buddy loved them; he loved the feeling of his stud in her tongue, rubbing up and down on his length made him cum quicker than ever. He also loved playing with the ring in her clitoris, making her cum time after time, drawing out her bodily fluids and licking her dry.

Lottie was petite but made-up with large breasts which her boyfriend loved. He was always fucking them, massaging the liquid into her large breasts later. He would make her come flicking his tongue on her clitoris.

When there were just the three of us together, we shared our sexual experiences, necking a couple of bottles of wine, laughing, and pretending to demonstrate some of the actions. The girls weren't serious with their guys, just using them when they wanted. God that would be nice, having a guy on tap with a click of your fingers, but I was jealous having to hear the pleasures of their experiences being on my own masturbating in my bedroom, hoping one day I would have a partner to share my experiences with.

'Liz, what the fuck have you been up to?' asked Emma and Lottie in unison as they looked at me.

'I'll tell you later. I've got to get ready for work and try and hide these love bites, so will you find something to cover them up? Will you, Lottie?' I begged sounding slightly desperate. While I dived into the shower, Lottie dragged out her large bag of cosmetics pawing through them, knowing what she was looking for. She worked as a PR in the cosmetic trade, which gave her loads of free samples, having to look her best at work. It was company policy and part of her contract to wear make-up at all times.

As I dried myself walking over into my bedroom to the full-length mirror, I stared at it. I couldn't believe what Jo had done to me, leaving his marks all over my body; it was as though he had marked me on purpose, stating as though I was his property. Lottie tottered into my bedroom with her bag of tricks.

'Wow, Liz, he's certainly marked you well,' said Lottie, surprised by the number of marks over my body.

'So, what have you got, Lottie?'

'Don't worry, I've got it covered. So, tell me what you are you wearing tonight?' she asked me animatedly.

'I'll have to wear something around my neck,' I started digging deep into my wardrobe and found sleeveless, silver top with a pair of black trousers. 'This will have to do; it gets that hot in the bar, especially tonight being Friday night, it will be packed.' I slipped them on while Lottie fixed me up, covering the marks that were still showing.

After getting ready, I checked in the mirror; she had done me justice.

'You should be a make-up artist for the movies.' I looked at her.

'I nearly went into that, but I love the job I'm in, not only that it pays well.' She waved her hand in the air dismissively.

'Hmm, point taken.' By the time I had a quick bite to eat, it was just before 6.30 pm. I left the flat, heading for the bar.

Lottie had done a good job covering my marks; I felt more confident serving customers without them staring at me. It was a busy night with a lot of newer faces coming in. I was being chatted up, and I was so overwhelmed with offers; I had never experienced so many in one night. Gosh, the choice was hard. As the night went on, I started to think who would be the lucky guy I was going to lay tonight? I narrowed it down to three guys. Fuck I can't, I've got all those love bites on my body underneath my hidden clothes, it wouldn't look right for them to see them knowing I had sex with someone else. Or could I, if we left the light off? Fuck it; I needed this. Jo and his mate hadn't been in. I suppose I was a little disappointed and would have liked a rerun of last night, but it wasn't to be; It was a tossup between Pete, Jamie, and Mark, all being of similar age of ten years older than me.

Pete was tall with messy dark hair and a couple of days growth on his face making him a bit rough for my sensitive parts but seemed bossy and too pushy, needing to be in charge of the situation. He seemed to me as though he was the sort to have you tied up and being a Dom, I didn't trust him in that situation, not knowing anything about him.

Jamie was tall with long dark hair that was smoothed back; clean-shaven with one pierced studded earring and one on the corner of his eyebrow, he looked sexy. Mark again was tall with short blonde hair and was cleanly shaven. I had now narrowed it down to Jamie and Mark. Jamie was drawing towards me having those piercings; I wondered if he had anymore I couldn't see. I needed to find out. It was getting on for 11.30 pm, with only half an hour to go. Jamie called me over, asking me what time I finished.

I told him that I was going to be free in half an hour. By this time, Mark and Pete had gone leaving Jamie on his own. They all worked together contracting for a local company but were staying in a flat temporarily until the job was completes, his flat was subsidized by the company, and he shared it with another guy who wasn't out with them tonight.

Midnight had arrived; I was off, leaving a remainder to the staff about clearing up. I was on a date with this guy and didn't want to keep him waiting. Walking in the opposite direction of my flat, I asked him where we were going.

'I thought you might like something to eat,' said Jamie. I was taken aback by him, not wanting to bed me straight away.

'Yes, that would be nice.' I smiled. A couple of hundred yards down the road was a takeaway. We didn't have to queue as the night was still young and no clubbers were spilling out from the clubs. I could now see Jamie in his tight jeans and tee-shirt showing his muscular body. I guessed his work kept him fit; his arms looked so strong. I noticed a large tattoo on his back as his tee-shirt raised slightly when he reached over to pay for the food. Fuck, this guy was turning me on, I needed to see more of his naked body, pressed next to mine. We walked further down the road crossing over down towards the embankment eating our food, chatting in-between each mouthful of food until we had finished.

It was going to be a great night. I could feel it in my bones.

Chapter Four:

Discarding the food containers, we walked further down to the embankment, then he took hold of my hand and pulled me toward him. Kissing me on the lips and tasting the food we had just eaten, he ran his hand under my top, cupping my breasts while his muscular arms snaked around me, squeezing me towards him. I could feel him hard against me, ready for some attention. God, I needed him, I thought getting aroused, so I began running my hand down towards his hardness. I undid his trousers with one hand while I ran my other hand through his long hair holding him tight.

We were both aroused due to our strong desire; I knelt down once I had taken his length out of his trousers and started licking his attention-seeking manhood. To my utter surprise, he had a piercing on the end of his length; this sight aroused me more. I sucked him hard with his ring tickling my tongue, while he stood there moaning with pleasure his hands on my head moving with the rhythm until he came. He shut his eyes and cried, shooting the lot straight down the back of my throat. I could taste his hot salty liquid in my mouth as I licked it dry. I stood up, licking my lips as he pulled himself together, fastening his jeans.

"Come on," he said, "let's go back to my place." We started running towards the flats I could see ahead. I was longing for him to enter me hard, and to go down and suck me dry.

"Shit I had forgotten the marks on my body; I'll just have to make sure the lights were out." I thought as I watched him walk to the door. Unlocking his flat door, he kissed me and cupped my breasts. Moving through to the bedroom after kicking the door shut, he started to undo my trousers as I kicked off my pumps, my trousers dropped down, leaving my lacy black undies. With urgency, I peeled off his tee-shirt. I could see in the shadows his muscular body and arms; I grabbed hold of his jeans unbuttoning them for the second time. He pulled them off as he peeled my top revealing my black lacy bra.

He unhooked my bra, and my breasts were released in all their glory; I was naked, and so was he. I pushed him onto the bed and straddled over him, kissing him hard with my breasts pressed against his chest. I could feel his strength as he took hold of me turning me over to straddle me, squeezed my breasts and sucked on my already hard nipples.

My wetness was exploding. Wrapping my leg around him, I felt his hardness again; he had soon recovered. He started to slide down, pushing my legs further apart and licking me until he was at my clitoris. He then pulled my lips back to drink in my wetness and rubbed hard on my clitoris with his thumb making me come twice, god, he was fucking good. After drinking me in, he moved up, slamming his length hard inside me. I felt his ring tickling me; the sensation was overwhelming; he kept making me come over and over again until he came with me. Fuck this didn't happen very often for me to get some pleasure.

I was in the same situation again, after having great sex all night with all that sucking and fucking, I left him asleep in the early hours, not knowing if I would see him again. Why do I put myself in such situations, and they always fall asleep on me? I wondered. Emma and Lottie weren't in when I got home at 7 am Saturday; I was on my own once again, not knowing about when would I get my next fix of sex.

Seeing that I had the place to myself, I headed for the bathroom to have a soak in the bath aching with having sex all-night with a guy I didn't know; he was pure lust. The piercing on his length was to die for. He also knew well how to press the right buttons and with his hard fit body pressing next to mine, I was in heaven, feeling his muscles working as he exercised his sexual exploits.

As I laid in the bath soaked in hot water daydreaming of my sexual exploits only a few hours ago, I heard the door in the flat open. Footsteps padded across the hallway towards the bathroom, the door opened as Lottie rushed in ignoring me in the bath going straight to the toilet.

"You look as though you've had a good night," I muttered.

"Yeah, just a bit. I went to a party with Jess from work and met some guys, and before we knew it they were supplying us drinks, and I think they spiked our drinks, so I don't really know what happened after that," said Lottie holding her head in her hands while she sat on the toilet with her pants around her ankles.

"Hmm sounds suspicious to me Lottie, do you think they jumped you then?" I asked.

"I think so, my boobies ache and feel wet. The trouble is none of us knows them, they seemed decent guys, but it just shows you can't judge a book by its cover, and I must admit we did drink a lot," said Lottie with another moan.

"Why don't you go to bed Lottie? I'll make us a coffee as soon as I've finished my soak," I offered.

"Yeah thanks, Liz" Lottie wiped herself and pulling her panties up, headed for her bedroom.

After my soak, I slipped on my silk robe, which hardly reached my knees and headed to the kitchen to make the coffee. There was a clicking noise of the key on the flat door and Emma came in looking fresh as a daisy humming to herself.

"You look happy." I smiled at her.

"Yes, Liz, I've got some news. Is Lottie in?" asked Emma.

"Yes, but she is a bit worse for wear. She thinks she may have had her drink spiked, and she can't remember much." I filled her in.

"Oh, dear poor old Lottie, for the first time in forever, she wouldn't know if she enjoyed it or not," said Emma sarcastically.

"So, Liz, what happened to you the other night when you came home with all those love bites?" said Emma sounding a little envious.

"That was Jo. He was waiting for me after I finished work at 11.30 pm and we headed straight to his flat." I winked. "We were going at it all night, I didn't want to leave, so that's why I was in a bit of a panicky, but I didn't know he had marked me that much until it was pointed out to me at work. God, it was so embarrassing, but I managed to keep away from the managers until 5 pm." I fanned my face with my fingers as I explained everything to Emma. "But last night I met Jamie he had the most wonderful piercing and made me come time after time, I couldn't leave him. But the only problem is that I only have the one-night stands, and I never see them again; even though they know where to find me if they were interested." I said, sounding disappointed.

"Aww Liz, you must shag the living daylights out of them, so they sleep like a baby when you go," said Emma patting me on the arm.

"That's the problem. When I leave them, I don't like to wake them since some people aren't morning people and I don't like rejection," I said slightly hurt.

"Oh, don't be daft Liz, you won't get rejected with a fit body like yours," said Emma trying to perk me up.

"Thanks, but what is so happy about then Emma?" I asked her.

"Well, I'll tell you both together when Lottie's sobered up." She smiled big.

"Ok, would you like a coffee while I'm making one?" I asked her guessing in my head what she might have to tell.

"Yes, please." Emma nodded. I finished making the coffee and took a mug into Lottie's bedroom. She was laid out on the bed fast asleep; I left her coffee on the side and closed the door behind me.

Walking into the living room where Emma sat drinking her coffee, I said. "Oh, Emma, come on spill the beans already." I was now desperate to know her news.

"Liz, I would prefer if you both were here, but ok, I'm bursting to tell someone," said Emma. "Well I have been promoted at work, and they want me to take over the department in the London office, there is a flat with all expensed paid, and I will be doing a lot of travelling," said Emma excited.

"Wow, Emma! I'm pleased for you, but that means you will be leaving us then?" I bet I sounded a little disappointed.

"Hmm, yeah, I know that's the problem, I've loved my time living with you both and the laughs we have had. I will miss that, but this promotion means a lot to me. I've worked hard for this, Liz," she said earnestly.

"Well, I'm pleased for you then Emma." I smiled feeling jealous as I compared her job with the job I had. In sales, you take the flak from some of the customers, but you get immune to it after years of doing a similar job, but I loved the new job I was doing.

"And what about Lee how serious are you with him?" I brought my attention to our conversation.

"Well, he is coming with me as he can get a transfer from his company to London." She turned slightly pink while saying this.

"I am really pleased for you, Emma. I wish my life would change, too. I seem to be in a rut with my job and the bar job meeting these guys but having no steady partner like you and Lottie, I'm so fed up."

"Liz, you have a fit body, and you're experienced in the sack, but a little advice I will give you, don't look as though you are needy with the guys, take charge of them in the sack. They do like to be bossed around a bit," said Emma raising an eyebrow.

"Yeah, I suppose you're right, Emma."

Lottie surfaced from her bedroom after 3 pm; she was still a little delicate but more human despite having her drinks spiked at some point during her evening out. Alan was due to come around tonight, so Lottie had to make herself feel a lot better, so she tottered off to have a shower to wash her hair and body of any signs and smell of whatever had happened last night.

The marks on my body were fading but still needed Lottie's experience with the make-up. Alan was coming round after 7 pm so I wouldn't see him, I thought to give Lottie time to patch me up. The weather was muggy, and the bar would be heaving with it being a Saturday night and live music. The mainly played the 80's and upwards. Jerry asked me if I would stay until 1 am he had a private party upstairs in the events room, which was mainly used for company conferences in the day time. I had no problem with staying over; it wasn't that I had anywhere to go and no one to share my time with.

The band was setting up as I arrived; walking across the dance floor I heard a wolf whistle from the stage area, ignoring it I walked straight into the back of the bar to hang my jacket and bag to reveal a black mini skirt and a short-sleeved white blouse knowing that I would be working upstairs. Bugger, I was going to miss hearing the band play, but at least there was music upstairs. The party didn't start until 8 pm, so I served a few customers before going upstairs. From the shadows of the stage, a guy dressed in jeans and a black vest top came over, looking as though he had just taken something, his eyes were moist and starring.

"Hello, darling. What's your name?" He looked at me.

"I am Liz. So, you're part of the band then?" I asked.

"Well, I'm just a singer," he said, being cocky. I was playing it cool, listening to what Emma had said not to feel so needy. "I'm Josh, lead singer of the band; we're called the 'Beat'." He smirked saying it with a swagger. "Are you going to have a drink with me then, Liz?" he asked, flashing wade of notes from his back pocket.

"I can have a quick one then as I am needed upstairs thanks." I shrugged.

"Oh, I wouldn't mind taking you upstairs." He smirked again coming out with the usual comments you get working behind the bar.

"Yeah, I bet you say that to all the women you meet." I rolled my eyes coming back with an answer.

"Only the sexy, fit ones," he replied as he ogled me up and down, I could imagine him stripping me naked with his eyes and wanting a good shag. But tonight, he was out of luck I was feeling a little low as to Emma's comment.

After having a quick drink with him while he stared at my legs and cleavage, it was time to go upstairs to serve behind the bar at the private party. There weren't many party-goers there when I arrived upstairs, it was mainly the older generation. Jerry had a buffet set out with the film wrapped firmly over the dishes in readiness for the influx of the party-goers when these would be peeled off. The music was slow, but as time went by, and people started to filter in the tempo changed to dance music. The floor began to fill, and so did the bar, I was starting to get busy being on my own, the younger guys made comments as I served, but ignoring their comments I just smiled; that's what you do working as customer service.

There was a lull at the bar, so I went to clear some of the tables off the plastic glasses, at least I had no washing up to do. A hand grazed my shoulder; I turned around to look who that was. Standing there was Gus, the guy I briefly met Friday in the staff kitchen at work. I hadn't taken any notice of him then as I needed to get out with my marks showing and trying to hide them, I needed a quick exit out of the building. He looked different out of his suit, wearing jeans and a black tee shirt now. His messy blonde hair and piercing blue eye made him look sexy.

“I didn’t know you worked here part-time,” said Gus surprised to see me.

“Yes, I work here three evenings a week, Thursday, Friday and Saturday.” I pushed my hair out of my face.

“So that explains why you were in a rush getting on of the door Thursday, I thought it was me,” he said with a smile; little did he know the real reason, so I went along with it.

“Yes, I was coming here.”

“Don’t you get tired working two jobs?” he asked. God if he only knew the truth of my exploits after my evening serving behind the bar.

“No, I don’t need much sleep,” I said as I started collecting the plastic glasses. He followed me around the room, collecting the plastic glasses coming to the bar and binning them in a large lined bin. I had to cut him short of serving customers; he waited at the bar waiting for me to finish.

"Liz, could I buy you a drink?" he asked politely.

"Yeah, thanks I'll have a beer." Pulling a perfect pint and a half of beer, I placed them on the bar, his eyes watching me while I worked.

"You're a very hard worker, Liz," said Gus scrutinizing my moves.

"Well, I do my best." I shrugged.

The music was loud as party-goers made an exhibition of themselves dancing with having drunk too much, spilling their drinks and tipping over tables and chairs. A couple more guys came over standing next to Gus. They were friends of his age. Having had too much to drink, they swayed as they approached the bar.

"Come on, darling, let's have a couple of pints here." One of the guys said.

“Haven’t you had enough?” I said, being firm.

“Oh come on darling I never have enough, especially when I am looking at you with those long legs of yours, I bet you’ll like to feel something in between them.” He laughed. Gus was about to butt in, but I got there first.

“Yes, and you’ll have my knee between yours if you don’t shut it.” My voice was firm and hard.

“Oops, the teacher is telling me off,” he murmured, but Gus took hold of his mate and guided him over to the seating area away from the bar. His other mate followed, leaving me to carry on serving.

It was now after midnight, and the party-goers were thinning out, leaving the ones who had too much to drink slumped in their chairs inebriated. I had been busy all night, so I started to tidy up despite the odd party-goers still there. I kept working around them until it was time for them to go. Gus had gone; I hadn’t notice due to being busy. After I was happy with the upstairs being clean and tidy, I went downstairs. It was after 1, I asked Jerry if he needed a hand with anything else, but the bar downstairs was nearly empty, with only the band sat in the corner drinking and laughing.

"No thanks, Liz, and thanks for tonight," said Jerry as he paid me for the night's work. Gathering my things, I headed off home.

As I stepped out of the bar, I could hear someone from the shadows nearby. I carried on walking, not taking any notice until the shadow appeared in front of me. It was Jamie from last night.

"I've been waiting for you," he said, sounding sober and meaning it.

"I was in the upstairs bar, there was a private function tonight, and I was asked if I would do the bar?" I said.

"Come on, let's go back to my flat," he suggested as he stood close to me, kissing me on the lips, teasing me to arouse me, so I give in to him. He tightened his arms around me, kissing me harder, his hand cupping my chin, and he stared me in the eyes. I started to remember the night before, and the ring on his length making me come over and over again. Resistance was futile I had to go with him. We hurried as for as the embankment where I first got down on my knees and sucked him off. As he opened the door to the flat, I had already undone my blouse ready to strip off; I could see Jamie's bulge waiting to be tamed.

We went straight into the bedroom, and within seconds we were both naked, his hardness waiting for attention as I fell on my knees to take his length.

He gasped as I took his full length into my mouth, feeling his ring on the end. He was about to come when he stopped me, pushing me onto the bed and spreading my legs wide open. Jamie pushed his fingers inside me, gliding them in with his thumb pressing hard on my clitoris, he was making me wet and licking me as I came. God, he was good.

He kissed my body with his mouth open and took hold of my breasts, cupping them and squeezing tightly, taking my hard nipples waiting for his attention between his finger and thumb pulling hard. I had my hands in his long hair holding tight as he was making me wet with arousal. He managed a few seconds before he couldn't last any longer. Entering me with his length slamming hard, he groaned. I was wet in anticipation feeling his fullness with his ring urging me to come with him.

I was relieved I didn't have to go to work in the morning being a Saturday, making the most of the early hours until daybreak we fucked hard. The atmosphere was intense, and the smell of bodily fluids was in the air.

I was facing the bedside clock when I woke; it was nearly 9 am. I was aching and ready for a coffee. As I turned over thinking yes, this would be the opportunity for him to ask me to see him again, but stretching my arm across, I felt an empty bed. I rolled over only to find that he was gone. I couldn't believe it.

Was I just a bad person? I asked myself, but then I heard someone in the kitchen, wrapping the throw over from the bed around me. I waddled over into the kitchen. There stood a fat guy with a shaven head, tattoos down his arms and legs in his underpants and a dirty vest top. He had just boiled the kettle, probably make a coffee for himself. He turned to look at me with his eyes undressing me as he smirked.

"I was wondering who he had in bed this time, making all that noise I could hear this morning?" said the fat guy as though this was normal in the flat. My heart sank, so I was just a number, I was feeling a bit jealous knowing what we had together, but now the bubble had burst as he was giving the same to other women. My face dropped; the fat guy saw the disappointment on my face.

"I'm sorry to tell you, but Jamie is a free spirit and shags anyone who's willing." He looked at me with a facial expression as if to say I told you so. I turned around, heading back to the bedroom. I wanted to cry, but holding it back, I tidied myself up, slipping my clothes on that I had on the night before and slipped out of the flat quietly. Why do I pick the wrong ones?

Walking down the road I felt used; no one wanted to stay with me, what was I doing wrong? It was nearly 10 am when I arrived at the flat, Emma and Lottie weren't in. I needed them to tell me why I couldn't find a guy for more than a night? To have a shag buddy to be there for you. Slamming the door, I stripped off my clothes and had a long shower crying my eyes out, why me?

Chapter Five:

After my shower and a lot of crying, I was finally cleansed off the smell of Jamie and the sex we had, so I felt better that I had got it out of my system. What bothered me the most was why I was feeling down with the thought of Jamie and other women? I was jealous, was I expecting too much? I knew that I needed to get a grip and not let it get to me and just live in the moment.

I was due for work at the bar for 6 pm, as it was a Saturday night, and probably it would be heaving with only the typical dance music playing. Feeling tired, I went to lay down thinking about work and that I would be on my feet all night, not only that but for the last couple of evenings, I lacked sleep.

I was woken by the door, slammed shut, and the clicking of heels in the hallway heading towards my bedroom. It was Lottie; she pushed the door open, looking to see if I was in.

"Oh Liz, Alan's found out about the party I was at, and someone who was there that knows him has told him a pack of lies," said Lottie bursting into tears.

"Lottie, I thought you weren't serious with him," I said lightly, trying to justify the situation.

"Well, I'm not, but it still hurts." She rubbed her nose as she sobbed further into her tissue. I put my arm around her to hug her.

"Aww, Lottie, if you had been here this morning, I felt crap finding out last night the guy I was with is a womanizer and picks up women to take back to his flat for a good shag. I was gutted hearing that, I would have rather not have known Lottie." I told her about my experience.

"Mm, that is awful, Liz." She now hugged me. "Emma told me this morning about her good news," said Lottie.

"Yeah its good but we will have to get someone to move in when she's gone, I just hope we can find someone as good as her." I went on.

"Hmm, just like you, Liz," said Lottie hugging me tighter.

"Aw, thanks, babes." I smiled.

Lottie perked up after a while; it was getting on for 4 pm I needed to get a bite to eat before leaving for the evening. Making a couple of sandwiches for both of us, we sat in the living room discussing guys in general, the pro and cons of keeping a guy. Lottie was way ahead with keeping a guy; I had no experience in that department, only having sex with more or less anyone I fancied on the night.

Did we need one-night stands or a guy for keeps? Then an idea occurred to me, and I spoke about it to Lottie.

"Lottie, I have been thinking about having a holiday, so what about going on a singles holiday for two weeks in Spain?" I looked at her. "Emma will be gone in three weeks. What do you think?"

"Hmm, I don't know. It all depends if I can get two weeks off at work," said Lottie sounding unsure.

"Well, think about it, it will be so much fun," I said, desperate for her to come with me.

I was leaving for work when Emma came in still humming and bubbly, she had told Lottie previously about her promotion and moving to London.

"Liz had a good last night?" asked Emma with a smirk knowing I hadn't come home last night.

"Yeah, sort of, I'll speak to you later I need to be off to work." I waved as I slipped out of the door.

Jerry was behind the bar when I arrived. Sarah and Jody followed me in, both wearing short skimpy black dresses showing the maximum cleavage with roman sandals laced up to their knees. They looked hot and would attract customers. I was wearing trousers, having worn a short skirt the evening before. While hanging my jacket and bag in the back room, I could hear Jerry making comments to the two girls about their choice of clothing.

The girls giggled as Jerry said something else I couldn't make out, but as I turned to leave the room, Jerry was at the door.

"Oh, hi Liz, I need to speak to all of you about the dress code." He went on.

"Why? is there something wrong?" I asked.

"Well, no, not really, but I'll tell you in a minute when you are all here."

Jerry went to the bar pulling three half-pints of beer while he told us to go and sit in the corner at the far end of the bar. I didn't know Sarah and Jody all that well, mainly because we were always busy and didn't have time to socialize or chat to find out more about each other, only that both of them worked at the bar full time and shared the serving of food.

Jerry had waitresses with other members of kitchen staff, with the eating area away from the main bar and dance floor. Jerry brought the drinks over, placing them on the table and sat down. We took our drinks and took a couple of gulps before placing it back on the table.

"So, what's this all about then, Jerry?" I asked, curious about what he was going to say.

"I have been thinking," he said. "I have noticed over a while you girls dress differently, like tonight you two are in a dress and you Liz in trousers. So we should have a uniform for working behind the bar, and I've come up with this," said Jerry sounding excited. "This should bring in more customers to the bar." He pulled out a large bag from under the other table and plunged his hand in to pull out a black silky basque together with matching neck collar, suspenders, and fishnet stockings.

"Wow, so does this mean a pay raise?" Jody asked him with a smirk.

"Well, yes and no," said Jerry. "I will base it on the night's takings, so if there is a sufficient increase in the takings, I will work out a percentage. How does that sound?" smiled Jerry.

"So will this start straight away if we say yes?" asked Sarah, not too sure about the deal.

"Yeah, I'll give it a try, let's have a look," Jody said as they grabbed the bags off Jerry. I stood up, taking the bag and headed for the back room to try the gear on.

Jerry had bought quality; the silk was smooth as I ran my fingers over the basque; the size was based on small, medium, and large having inserts of elastic, making it hug your body like skin. Once I had slipped it on, I looked into the full-length mirror. Whoa, this was a bit revealing, the basque had pushed my boobs up, making them larger and fuller, giving the maximum effect. Luckily I had covered up my marks, and the majority of them were gone. I thought if it made money and pull the guys, who was bothered?

Walking out with my heels on into the bar, I was whistled at as a guy had just come in and been served with a pint. Fuck I wasn't expecting customers this early; his eyes were on me as I walked up to Jerry at the far end of the bar. Jerry's eyes were as huge as saucers, not believing in what he was seeing.

"Fucking hell Liz you're going to make me rich. There will be a long queue at the bar waiting to be served."

Sarah and Jody came over smiling, seeing the transformation on me and how it looked. Jody grabbed the bag and, with Sarah, tottered off to the ladies to put their outfit on so as not to miss the attention of the guys that would be ogling them at the bar.

Jerry was pleased as he came up to me, thanking and hugging me. Jerry was married with a couple of kids; he was in his forties with dark hair having flecks of grey spreading from his temple. His wife was a well-groomed petite dark-haired woman, who always wore make-up and was pretty to look at. Jerry was smitten with her despite her spending his money. Wearing the new uniform didn't bother me despite his sudden shock after seeing me dressed up as he wanted. Jerry was a family man; it was the first time I saw him look that gobsmacked at a woman as he had seen a few sights over the years running the bar.

Jody and Sarah were giggling as they walked through the door into the bar. I must admit they didn't carry it off as well as I did, me being taller and slimmer, but they would still turn heads. We were ready as the customers started trailing in from outside, Jerry changed the tempo of the music to more with suggestive lyrics to the songs playing, making the guys looking at us to buy more drinks and chatting us up with sexual comments of what they would like to do with us.

The till kept ringing all night, Jerry's idea was working. A couple of hours into our shifts one of us had to go and collect the glasses, so we would all take it in turns, Jody said she would go first.

She pushed her way through as the bar was filling up quickly, the men ogling and grabbing hold of her, she managed to keep it together without too much trouble running the gauntlet. We were that busy not looking at faces as we just wanted to serve as quickly as possible with the volume of customers. I heard my name called a couple of times, but as I looked up, trying to see where the voice was coming from, but I couldn't focus on anyone in general. We all had guys leaning over the bar trying to touch our boobs as the night went on, they were consuming beer by the gallons with some unable to stand. Ben and Pete were on the door, having to extract them out, knowing that they wouldn't be buying any more beer and would be a hindrance.

It was my turn to run the gauntlet; I had never seen the bar this full, having to push through pressing my body against the guys some could feel my boobs pressing in their back making them turn around to grope me swaying their eyes not focused with the amount of booze they had consumed, they were easier to handle than the sober ones. I heard my name being called again. I looked around as a hand touched me on the shoulder, it was Gus dressed in jeans and a loose light blue shirt, he was looking rather handsome, his blond hair still messy making him look sexy.

He guided me to the bar with the glasses, where we found a bit of free space to talk briefly before serving.

"Liz, you look rather ravishing tonight." he raised an eyebrow and smirked at me.

I didn't know what to say, "Um, I'm sorry, but I have to serve." I said, leaving him standing at the bar, watching me serving the customers. I could feel his eyes undressing what was left of my uniform. I wondered if I was turning him on. I would love to fuck him, but he was a work colleague so that it wouldn't work out, and I would have to find another job like I had to before.

The bar was still heaving at midnight; Jerry asked if I would stay on for a bit longer until the evening died down, making it easier for Sarah and Jody to cope with the running of the bar. I said I would stay until the end; he gave me a hug thanking me for helping him out. It was after 3 am before we locked up for the night, we all were bushed, our feet aching with being on them all night. We sat down, having a coffee that Jerry had made for us, with a big grin on his face. He had been cashing up with the profits, way more than he had expected, and with the hours we had worked, he gave us an extra £50 bonus on top.

"Wow, I wasn't expecting this," I said, surprised with the amount he gave us.

"You all have done me proud tonight, girls, and I hope we have many more like this," said Jerry rubbing his hands with glee.

I finished my coffee and made my way to the ladies to change back into the clothes I had come in with, leaving my uniform in the backroom before setting off for home. Sweat had been pouring off with the heat coming from the number of bodies crammed in the bar. It was nice to be outside, feeling fresher with a slight breeze in the air. I was tired ready for my bed; the streets were empty with the odd car passing by. I heard my name being called and turned around as Jamie came out of the shadows; he was looking all sheepish as though he had done something wrong.

"Liz, I've been waiting for you; I was in the bar calling you, but you didn't see me," he said.

"Well, we were busy, you know," I said sarcastically.

"Yeah, you could say that. Are you coming back to my place?" he asked.

"You left me went I woke up last time, and I met your flatmate who filled me in on your string of women you have in your bed." I spat out.

"Liz doesn't take any notice of him; he's only jealous he's not getting any; that's why," said Jamie pleading with me. I must admit I wished he was my partner like Emma and Lottie.

My feet were killing me, but so was he, I was thinking of the pleasures of his experienced tongue and that piercing on his length reaching the spot. I gave in walking quickly back to his flat.

"You looked too sexy behind the bar tonight." He praised as he impatiently started undressing me. I kicked off my shoes, releasing my aching feet, and I could feel his arousal pushing from his jeans, waiting for attention. I slid down, undoing his trousers taking his length in my mouth, sucking hard, making him moan with pleasure as he grabbed my hair, pushing with the rhythm. He couldn't wait to fill my mouth with his hot salty liquid. I swallowed hard, licking the surplus from the tip of his length.

We laid on the bed naked; his length was still hard; my wetness was waiting for him to perform to my satisfaction.

"Liz," said Jamie as though he was about to confess. "The job we've been on finishes next week and will be moving on, but I'm not sure where yet. We haven't been told yet." My heart sank with the disappointment of not seeing him again. Straddling over me, he said, "well, I'll have to make the most of you then." he went down, leaving his hands squeezing my breasts and rubbing my nipples with his finger and thumb. My nipples hardened from the attention to the sensation, his mouth and tongue pressing hard on my clitoris starting to make me come.

I was about to come as he stopped climbing up with his mouth to my nipples, sucking hard. I felt his hardness on my body, ready to enter me. A few seconds, he was in penetrating me to the maximum fullness his ring hitting the spot, making me come straight away. His hardness was still going as I kept coming over and over again until he finally came.

"Gosh, I had never had sex like this." He muttered. We were sweating with the fast pace of sex, panting as we lay apart on the bed.

"Jamie, I love being with you," I said and then wished I hadn't said it thinking I was getting a bit clingy. Jamie was quiet; had I said the wrong thing by telling him? I sat up to turn around, finding that he was asleep; fuck, why did this always have to be me? I didn't know whether to go and leave him to sleep or to stay, hoping he would be there when I woke up in the morning. I took the first option, gathering my clothes to slip them on to leave him to sleep. I will make sure I would see him before he moved on and try to find out where.

It was gone 6 am when I got home; the flat was silent. I was tired, so I went straight to my bedroom, collapsing on the bed where I drifted off to sleep. I woke up with Lottie standing at the side of my bed; she was holding a mug of coffee; I stirred as she put the mug on the bedside table.

"Here I've made you coffee, you must have had a heavy night last night," said Lottie.

"Mm, you could say that." I yawned sitting up to drink my coffee, Lottie sat on the bed.

"What happened last night you've still got your clothes on from last night?" asked Lottie, smirking.

"We were busy, and Jerry asked us if we would wear these uniforms, he had got us?" I told her.

"Oh yes, and what was that something skimpy?" said Lottie joking.

"Yeah, you can say that again."

"No, never, you didn't, did you?" asked Lottie with shock.

"Yes, you have got it in one," I told her about the uniform and that it brought in the customers drinking more as they ogled us over the bar. Lottie's jaw dropped; she couldn't believe it. Then I told her about Jamie waiting for me and going back to his place to have sex and him falling asleep on me.

"So I came home flopped on the bed, my feet were aching, I was tired, and I couldn't be bothered to change."

After our chat I undressed and went for a shower, thank god it was Sunday, I wouldn't have made it into work I was knackered. Lottie was in the living room, sorting her make-up bag. I shouted through if she wanted a drink?

"Yes, please, Liz." A few minutes later, I was bringing the coffee through and handed one to Lottie.

"I've got to make some room in my bag; we are getting new samples on Monday to try, would you like some of this, Liz? Some of them I haven't used." She offered.

"Oh, if you're sure, I'll take some off your hands to make some room." Lottie's make-up bag was a small overnight case with holders and compartments designed for the cosmetics.

Lottie said she would cook tonight; there was only the two of us as Emma was staying with Lee. She was cooking something quick and straightforward; I wasn't feeling all that hungry; I just wanted to catch up on my sleep. Forcing the meal down, with not had anything to eat all day, I left Lottie to wash the pots while I headed to my bedroom for my bed, I needed my sleep.

The following morning, I was still feeling tired, dragging my butt out of bed to the shower for a quick refresher. I made it to work a couple of minutes before 8.30 am. I threw my bag on my desk while I went to hang my coat up. Nearly everyone in the office was working at their desks as I sat down, switching my computer on. While I waited, I went to make a coffee to wake me up, as comments in the office had started.

I was always getting comments taking it in my stride and giving it back; I usually had an answer for most of them. We were always bantering and taking the Micky out of each other, it just made the job more enjoyable with having to deal with some of the rude customers, but I was used to that working at the bar in the evenings.

5 pm had soon come around; the day had gone quickly as customers were phoning their orders through. We were given every Monday morning a list of items we needed to clear at a reduce cost, I did well, clearing nearly half the stock despite the fact we didn't get any bonus for doing so, but it was my job to sell. By the time I had finished with my last customer for the day, it was after 5 pm.

I quickly logged off, taking my mug into the staff kitchen to wash for the next day. I was coming out when I bumped into Gus dressed in a grey suit looking handsome with that hair of his, I didn't know how he got away with that as the company was fairly strict on personal appearance including hair, but I thought this was mainly the sales team having to meet the customers on occasionally.

"Oh, hello, Liz, it's nice to meet you with your clothes on," said Gus smirking. It was a good thing no one was around to hear else there would be gossip running full throttle around the office.

"Hi, Gus I was just going," I replied, trying not to meet his eye. I didn't want to get involved with anyone from work, not only that I didn't even know where he worked in the building, and I wasn't going to ask.

"You are working tonight?" he asked.

"No, I only work Thursday, Friday, and Saturday night. I'm sorry I have to go. Lottie's cooking tonight." I said, making an excuse to get away from him.

"That's a pity I was going to ask you out," said Gus sounding disappointed. As I brushed past him, I felt a connection that I had never felt with anyone.

"Sorry I've got to go," I said, walking quickly, heading for my coat and bag. I was out of the door before he said anymore. Walking home I was thinking about what he had said and the feeling of that connection as I brushed past him, he must have felt it as well. It was true that I would love to fuck him, but he worked for the same company, and I did not want to leave as I knew these things never worked out.

I could hear the music as I ran upstairs to the flat; Emma was home in her bedroom, packing her things.

“What’s the rush you’re not going for another few weeks?” I frowned.

“Change of plans. They what me down there this week,” said Emma rushing around the room, pulling open the drawers and throwing them on the bed.

“Oh, we haven’t even advertised for your room yet,” I said in dismay.

“Don’t worry about that. I’ll still pay my side of the rent,” said Emma.

“It’s not that Emma, we thought we would have one last night out before you left,” I said, sounding disappointed.

“Mm, I know, so you both will have to come over for a weekend,” said Emma. Lottie soon came in saying the same words as me. We would now have to sort out an advert to put in the window. I just hoped we would get someone like Emma and have a good laugh and still share sexual exploits.

Chapter Six:

We put an ad together; Lottie called in the coffee shop on her way to work the following morning. While I was at work, it somehow slipped out that we were looking for someone to move into the flat. Cathy started to quiz me about wanting a new flat mate. I tried to put her off telling her it wasn't my decision and that we had a couple of people coming around tonight who Lottie knew.

God, I'd never go to heaven! I thought. I hated lying, but it was much needed here since I didn't want anyone knowing my business at home with the lifestyle I had. I also didn't want anyone to know about me working part-time at the bar. There were none of my colleagues living in my area, and wouldn't go in the type of bar I worked at so my secret working at the bar was safe so far except for Gus.

He was the only one who had seen me at the bar, that too in the uniform we had to start wearing. I was relieved at least he hadn't said anything as no one had made any comments in the office. Gossip travelled quickly in the office; it was only the other week when we found out that one of the managers was knocking off the manager in the HR department; that said something about the HR department.

The following evening, I was thinking about Jamie, and how I had left him sleeping like a baby, early hours of that morning. Before he fell asleep, he said that his work was finishing and he would be moving on but didn't know where. Looking at the clock, I decided I would go around to see him and find out if he knew where he was going next. As I approached the flat, I could hear music blaring out. I banged on the door, hoping the door would open above the noise of the loud music. A couple of minutes later the door opened, it was Jamie's, flat mate.

'Hi. Is Jamie in?' I asked with a sweet smile. He opened the door wider for me to come in and said;

'Yeah, he's in his room.'

I stepped in, walking toward his room, and as I opened the door, I could hear groaning noises. Too late! As I opened it, I found Jamie on top of a woman with her red six-inch heels on and his length inside her making her groan in pleasure. My heart sank, seeing him with someone else; it should have been me in her place.

Jamie had seen me at this point. He only stared at me saying nothing which made it worse; I was just a number. I turned to see his flat mate near the door, watching me knowing I would be back soon. The bastard knew he had someone in there and did this on purpose. Without thinking anymore, I ran out of the door and kept on running until I couldn't run any more.

Deep down, I knew this was coming, but I was still crying now, why? It wasn't like me; I thought we had something special, what a fool I'd been even to think that I would make a difference.

I got back to the flat. Emma was still packing while Lottie was in the living room. I went over to her, sat down and cried my eyes out to her, explaining what had happened.

'Oh, Liz, you poor thing, that's awful,' said Lottie patting my head.

'I thought we had something when he was waiting for me. I've been so stupid thinking it could have been something else.' I sniffed loudly.

'Well he did say he was leaving, didn't he?' said Lottie soothingly.

'Yes, but that's not the point, he was shagging someone else. It's just seeing him with someone else. I wish I hadn't gone then I won't have known any different would I Lottie?' I mumbled while tears rolled down my cheeks. I could feel a huge lump in my throat; guess it was sadness.

'Yeah, I suppose you are right, Liz.' Emma came through as she heard me crying, Lottie filled her into what had happened.

'Liz, you need to learn to say no to these guys. Don't always go chasing after them, you will only get hurt,' said Emma being blunt. It wasn't what I wanted to hear, but she was right, I had to say no to these guys.

We were starting to get enquiries in to take Emma's place in the flat. Lottie and I needed to interview them, bringing out their personalities and habits to find the best flatmate to fit in with us. Within a couple of days Emma had moved out, we all said our goodbyes with hugs and kisses plus a few tears remembering the fun we all had together while living in the flat. Now there were just the two of us until we found someone else. The following week we started to see a flow of people some males as well. We needed a female as a male in the flat would not work for us.

Jerry let me have a night without wearing the uniform, giving me a bit of a breather, but Friday and Saturday were a must being the weekend. He knew the weekend was the busiest in the bar with everyone out, making the most of it. We were fairly busy, but I managed to leave just after 11.30 pm, having no one proposing me to go back to their place. Jerry had organized a live band Friday night.

I had to be there before 6 pm, and Sarah and Jody were coming later as they were working on the restaurant side. They also left late and worked without a break. I waited until they came in before changing into my uniform as I knew it would be a long night in heels. The band had turned up, so we unlocked the back door to allow them to offload their gear and set up to play.

The band consisted of four guys of similar age, having long messy hair with tight leather trousers and white vests; they looked a typical rock band. I started putting down the chairs and placing the beer mats on the tables. One of the band members came over asking for drinks, he reminded me a little bit of Jamie with the long hair pushed back, but without the piercings. I walked over to the bar to pull four pints of beer; he came across to pay.

'I was told that the bar staff wear these skimpy uniforms,' laughed the guy.

'Mm, where did you hear that from?' I asked him.

'Oh a mate of mine, he was working around here just recently said one of the girls was easy and gave a good blow job.' He winked.

‘Oh, really? What’s his name?’ I asked, now curious.

‘Jamie.’ said the guy. My heart sank, Jamie had been talking about me and the sex we had, the bastard.

I felt cheap, dirty and used; as a sex object. I was starting to get a name with guys passing my name around. It was 7 pm when Sarah and Jody had arrived; we took it in turns to change into our uniforms, leaving me last. I had to process what the band guy had said about being easy; was that how guys saw me? Slipping on my uniform and putting on a brave face, I walked out into the bar.

The band was tuning their instruments as people started to trickle in. The same guy from the band came to the bar.

‘So, you give a good blow job I hear?’ He said with his eyes fixed on my breasts.

‘What makes you think I do?’ I asked turning red.

'Well, Jamie said that she was tall and fit, so it had to be you.' He was still ogling my boobs. Cutting him short, I went on bluntly.

'Do you want another round of drinks?'

'Yes, please, and a blow job,' he blurted out, giving me the eye and a smirk. I felt like telling him to fuck off, but I couldn't. I was working, and it wouldn't look good. Serving him the four pints I sharply put them on the bar, spilling a little, I was annoyed. I took his money and slapping his change in his hand; I continued to serve customers for the rest of the evening.

'Liz, a guy, is asking for you,' shouted Jody from the other end of the bar.

'Yeah, I won't be a minute,' I yelled back thinking it was the guy from the band. He could fucking wait. About half an hour later, I walked to the end of the bar expecting to see him, but it wasn't him. It was Gus dressed in jeans and a black open-neck shirt looking handsome and sexy.

'Oh, I didn't realize it was you. I thought you were someone else.' I smiled reflexively as I felt pleased to see him.

'Yeah? And who would that be?' he asked, sounding a little jealous.

'Just one of the band members was being a pain,' I said shrugging it off. We had a brief chat while I served him with a pint quickly, having to serve more customers. I could see Gus watching me as I served, but not in a purvey way like the majority of the guys did. How could I go out with him while working for the same company? Although he was not working in the same department as me, he worked on the finance side of the company which explained why I had never seen him before until that evening in the staff kitchen. I couldn't take that chance, not only that I loved working in the sales department, but I also enjoyed flirting with the customers over the phone.

It was nearly 3 am before we had cleaned up and locked the doors. Jerry had made us all coffee and had brought them to the table, waiting for us. We were still making him good money as he gave us all an extra £100 on top of our wages for the night.

'You're doing us proud, girls, bringing in the crowds,' said Jerry with a big smile written all over his face. After I drank my coffee, I nipped off to change, leaving the pub after 3.30 am. After putting on my pumps, I was feeling more comfortable than my heels. I was lucky enough to have no one waiting in the shadows, even if there was, I would have turned them down, after having a pep talk with Emma and with the guy in the band.

I didn't know if Lottie would be in, having broken up with Alan. I peeped into her bedroom when I found that she wasn't there. I guessed she had either got back with him or found someone else. Taking off my pumps and dumping my bag on the side, I made my way to my bedroom peeling off my clothes and slipping in between the sheets. As soon as my head hit the pillow, I was asleep. I couldn't bother taking off my make-up, it would have to wait.

I slept well, and it was nearly 2 pm when I woke up. The flat was silent, and it felt weird being on my own, not hearing Lottie and Emma banging about. We still hadn't found the right person to replace Emma; we still had a few weeks left but didn't want to rush it and end up with a total bitch living with us.

Lottie turned up in the flat when I was in the shower. She came straight into the bathroom as I showered, we were fairly open like that, and that's how it was with Emma.

'So, what's new with you, Liz?' she asked, taking a seat on the toilet. I was just finishing grabbing the towel and wrapping it around me as I stepped out of the shower.

'Well,' I went on and told her about the guy in the band knowing Jamie and what he had said.

'That bloody cheeks, bastard!' Lottie fumed. I told her how I felt about it like I was used as a sex object.

'Aww, Liz, look at Jamie shagging that woman. What would you call him?' said Lottie trying to compare.

'Mm, I suppose so. Anyway, never mind about me, what have you been up to?' I asked her.

'Oh, I was at a party with one of our clients, and I met this guy and went back to his place, but he wasn't as good as Alan; still, I had a good time,' Lottie smirked.

I didn't have to be at the bar until 7.30 pm as Jody was coming in for 6 pm shift. There was no live music tonight only music playing through the speakers on a playlist. It was another busy night; I saw some new faces and many regulars. I was getting chatted up about what time I finished, I thought about what Jamie had told the guy in the band. 'No, I wasn't going to be easy.' I thought and rejected their advances and comments and avoided flirting.

I was at the till when I turned around to serve the next customer and saw Gus standing at the bar waiting for me.

'Hi.' I waved cheerfully.

'Is there somewhere we can talk?' asked Gus.

'Well, I'm due for a ten-minute break,' I said. I told Jody and Sarah I was having a break, Gus followed me to the back of the bar into the changing area.

'So, what do you need to speak to me about?' I asked, sounding curious.

'Liz, I would like to take you out for dinner one night,' said Gus.

'Why would you want to do that?' I asked, raising an eyebrow.

'I like you very much, and I would like to get to know you more,' said Gus taking my hand and stroking it with his soft fingers. His touch was gentle, and it was sending little tingles through my body.

'Gus, I like you very much, but I can't get involved with anyone from work. It happened last time in my job, and I had to leave. I love my job,' I said slowly, wishing he didn't work at the same place.

'Liz, I'm only asking you out for dinner,' he said, trying to convince me.

'Oh, Gus, you are making this difficult for me,' I murmured and shut my eyes. Ten minutes were up; I had to get back to the bar.

'Okay, just dinner then?' I said.

His face lit up instantly.

‘Good, how about Tuesday evening? I will pick you up at 7 pm,’ said Gus pleased as punch.

‘Ok, then but I’ll have to go now.’ I waved again leaving him with a big smile on his face.

Monday had soon come around; I was wondering if I would see Gus at work. Yes, I wanted him, but I didn’t want to forfeit my job if it didn’t work out. I dared not ask questions about him at work as they would definitely start to gossip and then it would snowball out of control. But still, it was only going to be dinner so no one would see us together.

The day went quickly with the phone ringing nonstop. I was running late with my last customer; they wouldn’t stop talking once I had taken their order. It was after I have managed to persuade them to purchase some of the reduced stock items on offer. There wasn’t much-reduced stock left as I had sold 90% of it myself; pity I wasn't on a bonus, but still, I loved my job.

It was nearly 5.30 pm, and I was finishing off in the kitchen with my mug ready for the morning. I heard the door open and felt a pair of hands on my waist; I turned around quickly to find Gus smiling at me. I stared as he kissed me on the lips. I was taken aback not expecting him to do that, especially at work, not knowing if everyone had left for the day.

'Gus, stop it someone might come in,' I said in a panic.

'Nah, there might be the odd management left, but they wouldn't come down here,' said Gus holding up his hands in defence.

'Well, you never know who's around, and I don't want to take that chance, any way you didn't ask me where

I lived, seeing that you are taking me out tomorrow,' I asked.

'Didn't have to as you know what the gossip is like in the company. Everyone knows you and your flat mate are looking for another lodger and that you have an advert in the coffee shop with your address,' said Gus with a laugh.

'Ok point taken smart arse, anyway I better go,' I said, giving him a quick peck on the cheek as I rushed out of the staff kitchen to collect my things for home.

When I eventually got home, Lottie was waiting for me.

'Liz, we have someone coming around in a few minutes to see the flat. She sounds really nice on the phone.' Lottie sounded excited. By the time I had taken off my jacket, the doorbell rang. Lottie rushed to open the door.

'Hi yeah, I'm Alice. I phoned this morning,' I heard a female voice.

'Hi, come on in Alice,' said Lottie. I was in the living room as they both came through; Alice came over as bubbly and very chatty type of a person. After further questions and over an hour later, Alice left.

'Bloody hell, Liz, I thought she was never going leave!' said Lottie in exasperation.

'Hmm, so what do you think, Lottie?' I rubbed my hands together, sinking deeper into the sofa.

'Well, she comes across alright and seems to be very open with everything, plus she is single as well so at least we all have that in common,' said Lottie smiling widely.

'So, it's a yes then?'

'Yeah, I think so,' said Lottie. Lottie phoned her with the good news; I could hear her shouting with excitement down the phone. It would be at least four weeks before she could move in, mainly because of her changing her job and giving notice from her other job.

'Liz, you mentioned last week about going on a single holiday together? Well, I'm up for it, and my boss says I can have a couple of weeks off within the next few weeks as there is no one on holiday. So what do you think about going before Alice moves in?' said Lottie.

'Wait, what? That's brilliant. I'll have to sort it out at work, and I'll see what's available online.' It was decided to book what was available with work giving us an opening.

Tuesday morning, I went into work early, only to scour the internet for a good deal on our holiday. I found one leaving on Sunday; I had to phone Jerry, he wasn't very happy as he would have to find someone to cover for two weeks, not only that someone who would wear the sexy uniform. Lottie's boss was ok with her, and Matt, my boss, was too.

'Lookout Corfu, here we come!' I was so excited.

I made sure I left on time with Gus picking me up at 7 pm for dinner. I just didn't know what to wear, sexy or casual. I decided I'll go with a short black dress. The doorbell rang, Gus was early, and Lottie had gone out for the evening. I opened the door in my skimpy lightweight robe, Gus stood there looking handsome in black chinos and white open-necked shirt with a black jacket, his hair still looking messy but sexy as hell.

He handed me a bunch of red roses. I was taken aback; no one had ever given me flowers; all they were after was a hard fuck or a blow job. I thanked him, kissing him on the cheek as he followed me through into the kitchen to find a vase for the flowers.

'I'll sort these out; you get yourself ready,' said Gus taking hold of the vase. I padded off to my bedroom and slipped my black dress on having already applied my make-up.

Gus was waiting in the living room as I came out, god fuck the dinner I could fuck him instead, but no that would be wrong. He was a work colleague, and that could make it awkward.

'You look nice, Liz,' complimented Gus walking into the living room.

'Thanks, you scrub up well yourself,' I complimented back as we walked down the steps to the car. I was expecting a basic model that every normal person earning a living drove, but there parked on the roadside was a Porsche 911. My eyes lit up;

'Accounts must pay well,' I said with a bit of sarcasm.

'It's a friend of mine. He said that I could borrow it if I wanted to, I'm also staying in his flat until he gets back, he works abroad as an engineer in Saudi. They pay well.' said Gus trying to convince me.

'Mm nice, I thought you were being a flash git having everything but nothing,' I said, lifting my dress to get into the car showing more skin on the legs. Gus was quiet for a few seconds. He pulled out into the road heading towards the end of the city as he started chatting, asking me about my day.

We arrived just after 7.30 pm pulling up into a car parking full of posh vehicles. We walked into the restaurant where we were shown to our seats. The waiter handed us a menu; I noticed there were no prices.

'Gus, you don't have to impress me, let me pay half,' I said. 'I am not worth it; you know this can't go anywhere.'

'Liz, don't worry about the money. I'm single and have saved my pennies,' he said with a smile trying to lighten the conversation.

'Well, we could have gone to McDonald's. I don't like the thought of you spending money on me.'

'I like you; can't I take a colleague out and spend some of my hard-earned money on you?' said Gus dismissing what I was saying.

The conversation came easy; we bantered with each other, telling each other jokes. I had nearly drunk a bottle of wine; Gus just had a glass with having to drive. My tongue was starting to run away, slipping out that my ex-flatmate told me I was a needy person and that I needed to say no to men taking advantage of me. Gus sat there, listening to every word I was saying and said.

'Liz, have you been in love with anyone?' I thought for a few moments,

'No, they don't give me a chance.' Then realizing who I was talking to, I went on. 'Oh, Gus just forget what I'm babbling on about. It's the wine talking.'

I made a miserable attempt to finding an excuse for what I was saying. Gus didn't say anymore and changed the conversation to general. I told him I was going on holiday Sunday for two weeks but omitted to tell him it was a singles holiday with plenty of sex.

Chapter Seven:

It was nearly 11 pm when Gus finally brought me home. It had been great fun, so while sitting in the car parked outside the flat, I went on.

'Well, Gus, I must say I enjoyed tonight and thank you.' I kissed him on the cheek.

'Yes, I have, too. Very much,' said Gus smiling. He looked as though he wanted to say more but didn't.

'I would ask you in, but I need my sleep.' I yawned as I opened the car door, but then I stopped to turn and kiss him on the lips. As his hand cupped my cheek, I felt a tingle go through my body, there was something about him, and I just wished we didn't work at the same company. I watched him drive off as I stood on the steps.

Do I take that risk? I asked myself.

The rest of the week went quickly; I didn't see Gus at work at all. The sales team was busy with me selling off the remaining reduce stocks, meeting the sales department's target for the week. Matt, my boss, thanked me for my efforts in the surge to sell the clearance stocks to leave room to acquire new ranges. The bar was also busy Friday and Saturday night, and I had to leave after 3 am. I had many offers of seeing guys after work, as tempted as I was, I needed to pack for my holiday with Lottie having to be at the airport 10 am Sunday. We had to be there 2 hours before we boarded, so by the time I got home and finished packing and checking that we had everything we set off for the airport.

I managed to get some sleep on the flight after being on the go for over 18 hours. Coaches were waiting for us at the airport to take us to the hotel, dropping off passengers at various hotels along the way. We seemed to be on the coach for ages wishing for our stop to come sooner. Travelling further out of the town, I was frustrated, thinking about what had I booked? As with last-minute bookings, it didn't tell you the hotel you were staying at, only the star rating, which was a three which meant average.

The coach was approaching the edge of the town, and we were hoping that this was the last drop off point. The town was busy with many holidaymakers sitting outside the bars and cafes; there were many to choose from including night clubs advertising free drinks on entry to entice you in, others having happy hour at reduced rates. We were nearly coming out of the town when the coach stopped outside a five-star hotel.

'Bloody hell, Lottie, at this rate we will be pinching in a tent,' I said, getting fed up with travelling. I was tired of being up for nearly 20 hours with very little sleep. Then the courier called our names, I looked at Lottie, thinking she must have us mixed up with someone else. I got up shaking Lottie as she couldn't believe we were getting off the coach to a five-star hotel. There were only the two of us, with four couples left on the coach. I could bet they were sick of travelling with us from the airport, too.

While dragging our cases into the reception area of the hotel, we were stared at by other people staying at the hotel. We checked in with the receptionist asking the porter to take us to our room. He picked up our cases, and we followed him through the corridors of the hotel until we reached towards the backside that led into the garden.

Where the hell was he taking us to? Passing a couple of swimming pools, down the path to finally coming

out amongst some trees, we saw the villa.

'Bloody hell, Lottie, we have a villa to ourselves,' I said with a big smile. The porter unlocked the door, taking our cases in. Once he had gone after we had tipped him, we opened the curtains and blinds to be dazzled by the sun coming through. We stepped out on the balcony; the view was superb overlooking the sea. We had access from the balcony down to the beach.

I needed some sleep and so did Lottie before we hit the town that evening, so we left our cases and went to lie on our beds for a couple of hours. It was nearly 10 pm when we woke up. After the much-needed sleep, we were fresh now, and both of us were starving. We found our way around the town, finding a decent bar to get something to eat before hitting the nightlife.

The music was blaring out from nearly every bar in the street, playing mainly dance music with touts giving you a leaflet offering you a free drink inside their bar or nightclub. Taking the plunge with offers of a happy hour, we went into one of the clubs, which was heaving with clubbers. Half were already drunk, with guys coming up to you grabbing you and pretending to shag you, as they swayed back trying to keep upright. We stayed out until 2 am, but then travelling had caught up with us despite having some sleep. We decided to call it a night and headed back to our hotel.

It was after 10 am when we woke, feeling wide awake, I headed for the shower to freshen up. Lottie had started to unpack, waiting for me to finish with my shower. We had both missed breakfasts, which they finished serving at 10 am, which didn't matter as both of us weren't hungry. Once showered and unpacked, we ventured into the reception area of the hotel where our holiday rep sat in a corner near the bar.

We thought we would ask about why we were in a five-star hotel and not in a hotel with singles. She saw us coming over and waved.

'Hi, my name's Annie. I'm your rep while you are here for the next two weeks.' She explained why we were in this five-star hotel. 'Basically, the tour operator had double booked, and then one of us had to come here, but we wouldn't miss out on the action,' she said, giving us an itinerary for the two weeks. It was action-packed if you could stand the pace from partying on the beach to a wet tee shirt competition.

After a lengthy discussion with the rep, we headed for the pool, sizing the people staying in the hotel on the way. As we approached the pool area, we spotted four guys sitting on loungers drinking beers and laughing until they saw us. Next to the pool was a bar serving drinks all day and if you needed anything to eat you just had to ask the barman, and he would sort it. As we were being served, a couple of guys came up; they were just the average looking guys with the other two being more fanciable.

'Hello, ladies. Would you let us buy you both a drink?' asked one of the guys.

'No, thanks, it's ok,' I said, thinking if we did, we would be stuck with them.

'Oh, come on, girls we're just being friendly,' one of them insisted.

'Ok, then I will have a beer thanks,' I said just to shut them up. Lottie gave me the eye as if to say what I have done, by leading them on? With our drinks in hand, we walked around the pool to the other two guys. On a closer look we realized, they were a lot more handsome, both were identical twins with dark curly hair, slim build with blue eyes, they looked fit. I nudged Lottie and whispered 'Fancy shagging twins, Lottie.?'

'Mm, I know what you're thinking Liz, but what about the other two?' whispered Lottie seeing that they had bought the drinks.

'We can do them all if you want with some drinks,' I whispered back.

'So, girls have you got names?' one of the guys who had bought drinks asked.

'Liz and Lottie,' I said.

'Ahan? This is Jon, Pete, Cal and Lou.' They asked us how long we were staying and where we lived to give us the third degree, so I butted in asking them the same. I was surprised to find out that all of them were from our area living in the posh end of the city. They were all mates working in finance in the city centre. Our glasses were always full as they kept topping our drinks. I was feeling relaxed and flirty as did Lottie, so the guys moved forward, asking to go back to our villa. What the hell, why not? I looked at Lottie, who nodded with a smirk.

We stumbled back to the villa, and as we opened the door, the twins grabbed us, taking us into the bedrooms as the other two, one of which went with the other twin with Lottie while I had the other. Fuck! Both of us were going to have two up. I could hear Lottie giggling whatever they were doing to her she was enjoying it.

Cal started peeling off my vest to reveal my bare breasts as he cupped them, squeezing them hard. Jon was behind, pulling my shorts down; I was now naked not wearing any underwear, the two guys quickly stripped off as they released their hardness. Cal pushed my head down onto his length forcing me to suck him while Jon entered me from behind cupping my breasts, squeezing them tight until they hurt, this I hadn't experienced before having a two up.

They were forcing themselves, and I was gagging slightly before he came shooting all his hot salty liquid in my mouth. Jon pushed hard, moving me forward; I had to hold onto Cal for support until he came. I didn't enjoy it at all; it was just rough sex. When the guys had finished, they slipped their clothes on and left without saying a word, leaving me naked. I sat on the bed thinking, fuck I had been used as a quick fuck and entertainment for those guys. Were they trying to see how many they could shag while they were here? Within a few minutes, the other two guys came out of Lottie's bedroom and left without saying anything. I slipped my lightweight robe on and padded over into Lottie's bedroom; she was laying there with blood on the bed covers.

'Lottie, are you ok?' I asked, worried about seeing blood on the sheets.

'Yeah, they fucked me so hard it started my period which I knew I was due to start,' said Lottie sounding disappointed.

'I'd never experienced a two-up before, have you, Lottie?' I asked.

'Yeah, a couple of times,' said Lottie. I was shocked.

'You've never said.'

‘Well it had never come up in a conversation,’ said Lottie sounding nonchalant.

‘God, if that was two up, it didn’t do anything for me; I had no feeling of arousal with pleasure.’

On the itinerary the rep had given us, tonight was wet tee shirt competition night which was being held in one of the night clubs in the town. We both showered and after a change of clothes, we went to the nearest bar for something to eat, followed by a few drinks from various bars before heading down to the night club. We both were dressed in shorts and a tee-shirt, with no underwear; it was a hot and sticky evening.

The club was heaving with music so loud you couldn’t hear each other speak, so we had to mime to each other for communication. Everyone was friendly, kissing each other as though they knew everybody. We joined in getting into the party mood, frolicking on the dance floor, the music was good with the heat rising with the number of bodies in the club touching each other.

It was nearly midnight when the music stopped, marking the beginning of the wet tee shirt competition. Volunteers were needed on stage for the competition; both Lottie and I went up together with a few more as we were cheered and whistled at. Each one of us was asked a question if you got it wrong, you had water thrown over you, giving you a wet tee shirt to show if you were wearing a bra underneath. The first round of question all of us got right, but after the second round, two had wet tee shirts. The crowds started cheering and whistling, showing that the two girls had no bra underneath showing the outline and size of the breasts and nipple poking through the wetness of the tee shirts.

When the last round came, there was just Lottie, and I left, but the questions were hard. We knew that we would be beaten having a wet tee shirt in the end. Lottie had the largest breasts on show through her wet tee shirt sending the guys in a frenzy wanting to grab her off stage.

The music started picking up to full-throttle on the sound, I managed to sign language to Lottie where I was going, but she was busy necking it with a guy. I headed off to find the loo squeezing past hot bodies. I had to queue but not for long, as I came out, I had to run the gauntly back through the crowd and try to find Lottie, but it was like trying to find a needle in a haystack, with the club being jam-packed.

All of a sudden, I was grabbed around my waist from the back. I turned to find it was one of the twins from the hotel we were staying in, but before I could say anything, he kissed me hard on the lips holding me tight. I could feel his length rubbing against me. He looked at me and smirked having that dirty look as sex was on the cards. He started kissing my neck as his hand started to cup my breast underneath my tee-shirt; he was starting to arouse me. With one arm around his neck, I started to rub his length with the other.

He was well ready to come, dragging me from the crowded club, he headed for the door, and he hadn't spoken a word until we were outside the club.

'I'm sorry about this afternoon. It was the other two guy's idea to have a two-up, it's been their fantasy and put you two to the test if you both would go through with it,' he said apologetically. This one from the twins was Lou as there was a slight difference in the hairstyle. 'Come on, let's go back to my room,' said Lou starting to walk towards the hotel.

'Hang on a minute, how do I know this isn't a set up with the four of you?' I said as I tried to pull away.

'No, Liz I'm not really like that. We did have a bit to drink; I am sorry, Liz. It will only be just me and you,' he continued trying to convince me.

‘Ok, then on one condition, you come back to our villa instead of me going to your room,’ I said.

‘Yes, wherever you feel comfortable with.’ We headed back to the villa. He kept touching my butt and kissing my neck, arousing me on the way; I could feel my wetness coming through. As soon as the door was opened, our clothes were off, on the floor. He was inside me pushing hard as he couldn’t wait and within seconds had shot his lot. I was half expecting him to leave, but he didn’t. A few seconds later, we got up naked; as I saw his fit body, he was still hard, I approached his length, taking it into my mouth and started to suck him hard.

He stood there with his legs slightly apart moaning with pleasure; his hands were on my head working with my head to the rhythm until he finally came. I licked him clean, making my way up to his body to his lips, kissing him hard. His arms snaked around me, moving to my breasts squeezing hard. We were sweating with the hot night and sex.

We headed to the shower for a cold shower, to clean off the sex we just had. After we had showered, I went to the chiller in our room for a bottle of cold water, knocking half the bottle back with thirst. I handed him a bottle as well, which he drank it down in one.

We went to the bedroom, and we both laid on the bed in silence. I noticed he still was hard and had to ask the question why.

'You must have a good sex drive?' I asked.

'Why do you ask?' said Lou.

'Because you're still hard from the time when we left the club, and it hasn't gone down yet,' I said telling it straight to the point.

‘Mm, I’ve had a little helping hand with some pills.’ Cal gave me his secret. ‘It keeps you hard for a few hours,’ said Lou.

‘I like the sound of that,’ I said, turning over to straddle him inserting his length inside me, it felt good as I sank wriggling to feel the fullness of his length. He pulled my nipples, making them tingle in pleasure as my wetness started to come. The sex was hard, but he was not coming with me, I was a bit disappointed, and I wanted a guy to pleasure me and to come together.

It was gone 10 am when I was woken up by the bright sunshine beaming through the slits in the blinds; the bed was empty, which I was expecting, they never stayed. God, I had forgotten where Lottie was. Getting up in a panic, I padded over to her bedroom. On pushing the door open, I found her in the clutches of a fit guy having sex despite her period. I left her to it while I went for a shower.

Half an hour later Lottie came into the bathroom while I was drying my hair, she looked shagged out.

'Lottie, I don't know how you can have sex when you're having your period, I could never do it,' I said, wrinkling my nose.

'Well, when a girl wants it, she gets it no matter the situation you're in, any way it's only going to be another couple of days,' said Lottie grinning. I was pleased that mine wouldn't be until we got back.

'So, who was the guy then?' I asked.

'Oh, some guy from the club, he's staying in one of those single's hotels where we should have gone. He says it's basic and the food is crap having to eat out. When he saw this place, he didn't realize we were on the single's holiday as well.'

'So, are you seeing him again?' I asked.

'Depends if we bump into each other,' said Lottie waving her hand not really bothered. She had soon got over Alan ditching her; she was moving on with her crusade bedding as many guys as she could. Lottie showered while I slipped on shorts over bikini bottoms and a yellow vest ready to venture out into the heat of the day.

When we left our villa, the maid had just turned up to clean, Lottie had stripped the bed ready for clean sheets to be put on, and I should say that she would have seen all sorts irrelevant of what star hotel it was. We headed to the bar where we had eaten the previous day. After our meal, we walked along the streets heading towards the beach. It was heaving, with some females topless exposing their breasts as the sun burned their skin to blend in the rest of their bodies. Most were wearing tiny bikini bottoms with ties at the sides, which could be easily slipped off with a tug. I had the same type of bikini bottoms mainly for that reason if the opportunity arose for easy access. Lottie had gone for the G-string; she had a nice firm butt, and she used it to her advantage together with her large breasts.

We stripped off our tops to expose our breasts, paddling along the seashore, just heading to see how far it took us. Some of the older generations looked on, shading their eyes from the sun. It wouldn't have mattered if we were stark naked feeling the heat of the sun on our bodies, it would have been nice to bare all, but the beach only allowed topless. We must have walked a mile before we came to a bend on the beach. The area was fairly sparse with buildings, but as we slipped through a narrow gap in the rocks, we were in for a surprise. We had stumbled upon a cove with a beach and a bar area.

But the best thing of all, the people were totally naked. I stripped off feeling free as the sun rays could now reach every part of my body. I was surprised that Lottie did the same; she pushed in her string to her tampon, so it didn't show, she was very confident not letting anything get in the way. As we approached the naked bodies, we noticed that they were of a similar age group with a few slightly older. Everyone was friendly as we started chatting, it turned out they were mainly on the single's holiday, the conversation turned to the itinerary for the week in which we found out that it was repeated every week.

We were chatted up from all angles, offering us drinks in which we accepted, why not? We knew what they were after. We noticed some of the guys and girls heading off towards the other side of the cove, both of us were asked if we wanted to go, so we followed. The other side led in an area of dunes as far as the eye could see, and couples disappeared in between them as they paired off.

I was led off by a tall, dark guy with long hair, slightly reminding me of Jamie and the piercings. Lottie had paired up with a guy with a shaven head but very muscular. We separated going our separate ways to find a free sand dune. We headed towards the seashore as we both needed to cool down with the heat. Waist-high in the sea, he grabbed hold of me, cupping my breasts and squeezing as he stood close behind me kissing my neck, making me come alive. I could feel he was all ready to enter me. His hand moved down to stimulate me with his fingers; he pressed his thumb as he found the right spot making me come at once.

It was nice to have that feeling with a guy, at last, he seemed to be in no rush. He turned me around, and I jumped onto him as his length entered me. I could feel the full penetration of his length as he worked me onto him. It was good, but within a few seconds, he had come inside me. We stayed linked together for a few minutes before parting away.

We walked further down the beach, splashing and pulling each other into the water until finally, we came to an area of grass where we flopped onto the ground. The heat soon dried are bodies, I rolled over to straddle him moving down to take in his length in my mouth. I teased him with my tongue flicking the end, making it stand to attention ready for the next stage of pleasure. Taking his full length. I sucked him hard as he moaned with pleasure, placing his hand on my head, grabbing hold of my hair to go with the rhythm. As he came, I swallowed his hot salty liquid in one go, after which I licked the tip for the last few drops. He flopped back to the ground as I came up kissing his whole body and sucking hard in places until I reached his mouth, I pressed hard on his lips, he wasn't forthcoming with kissing only on his terms. I pulled away to get up.

Where are you going?' he asked.

'I'm going back,' I said. He wasn't playing ball; he wanted it on his terms. I won't be letting it happen again. Now, I will play on my terms.

Chapter Eight:

I picked my beach bag, pulling out my shorts and slipping them on I headed off back to the cove. I needed a drink as I was fuming. Why was he making it a big deal? Was I asking too much? Why is it just sex always? I suppose that's what the guys want, just sex with no meaning. Was I expecting anything different this time? Well, whatever it was, was not working anymore or I was getting the wrong type of guys.

I couldn't see Lottie anywhere; she must be having a better time of it than me. I bought myself a beer and knocked it back in one; it was starting to get late in the day as the sun was going down and the heat wasn't as fierce. An arm wrapped around my waist as I was about to buy another beer. Startled, I turned back to look; it was Lou from the hotel.

'Hello, Liz, you've found the cove ok, then?' he asked casually.

'Yes, you could say that,' I said taken aback a little as he had only got out of my bed a few hours ago and was acting as though it hadn't happened.

'Here let me get that.' He said, pulling a note from his back pocket and handing to the barman.

'Thanks, so what are you up to?' I asked as I could see him on his own.

'Oh, I thought my brother and my mates were down here, but I found you instead.' He closed in kissing my neck and working down to my breast.

The barman didn't bat an eyelash; he must see this all the time having couples fornicating in front of him. Feeling Lou's hardness against me, I pulled him around to the back of the building where we both whipped off our shorts. There was a bench at the back; I pushed him onto the bench as I straddled him. I was going to be in charge this time; I wanted him to come at the same time as I. Feeling his full length inside me, I rode him as he squeezed my breasts pulling my nipples, my wetness was growing as I was about to come, but he spoilt it by coming before me.

'Fuck sake Lou couldn't you wait for a little? I was nearly there.' I was annoyed with him.

'Sorry, but if a guy's got to come, he can't stop,' said Lou; as if to say tuff I've got what I wanted. I stayed straddled over him, his length still inside me. I began rubbing my clitoris, masturbating to finish my pleasure which he had not given me.

I dismounted him as he laid there half expecting me to take him in my mouth. Bollocks, he can fuck himself. I thought as I picked up my shorts and bag. I walked off, heading towards the sea to wash off the sex I just had in the last couple of hours with two guys, both failing to give me any satisfaction. They just wanted to offload to have their pleasure. The sea was soothing; my skin had started to tan slightly. I smiled thinking that by the time we went home, I would have a lovely deep tan all over with no white bits to show.

There were still no signs of Lottie as I headed back to the end of the cove. I looked around slightly annoyed having to put on my shorts as I had approached the topless beach only. It was another hour before I was back at the hotel. There wasn't anyone in the pool, so I took the opportunity to have a dip. I plunged into the pool with what I was wearing, seeing that the villa was only a hundred yards away. The water was cool, and it soothed my skin from the day's sun. I swam for half an hour fuming that guys were getting what they wanted, but I wasn't. I swam hard to get the frustration out of my system.

After the lengths I had done, I sat on the side of the pool leaning back on my elbows, with my eyes closed, immersed in my thoughts for a few seconds before I heard a man's voice say.

'I take it you have had an argument with someone for swimming like that?' I opened my eyes, trying to focus where the voice was coming from. I looked up as the guy blocked the sun from my eyes, I could see him now; tall slim toned body and a nice tan.

'Yeah, you could say that,' I said sounding a bit off.

'So, do you want to talk about it?' he asked, sounding sincere.

'Mm, I don't know.' I shrugged.

'I'm a good listener, and I need a friend. I've just separated from my wife,' he said, pulling a face.

'Why not?' I thought. 'Can it get any worse with the guys just wanting a fuck?'

‘Your room?’ I said, gathering my things and still soaking wet, we headed to his room in the hotel.

His room was really plush having a drinks chiller with a selection of drinks; he said I could use his robe after getting out of my wet things courtesy of my spontaneous swim in the hotel pool. The bathroom was large, having a massive walk-in shower and a bath to match. As I came out of the bathroom, he had poured two glasses of wine which were stood on the coffee table in the room next to the sofa. Sitting next to him, I grabbed a glass taking a couple of gulps to quench my thirst and then leaning back onto the sofa I went on.

‘God, I needed that.’

‘I’m Luke by the way.’ He said, keeping his hand on his chest.

‘I’m Liz.’ I smiled slightly.

‘So, Liz, tell me your problems.’ he sat back waiting for me to start talking. Taking another gulp, I started telling him about what was on my mind.

‘Why do guys just want what they want and not what the girl wants? I started. I was blabbing on about my work and about what Dave had said to me when I didn’t meet him that night, and then why I had to leave my job as the atmosphere was tense. The guys I had picked up from working at the bar, I poured it all out, he didn’t know me, but for some reason, I could fill him in with my sex life, probably because he was married and I wouldn’t see him again.

After I had finished babbling on, I knocked back the last few mouthfuls of wine and put the empty glass on the coffee table. Luke poured me another glass of wine. He also had drunk full of his glass but still topped his glass up.

'Liz, what you need is the pleasure which these guys aren't giving you; you want to make love, explore each other's bodies and come together.' He was right in one; he seemed to understand what I needed.

'You're right, how do you know that?' I asked, looking at him with my head ducked to one side.

'Mainly because I've been married for ten years.' He said.

'So, what happened?' I asked, being nosey.

'I cheated on her with her best friend,' he said.

'Ouch,' I said; 'this sounds familiar to Dave, but at least we didn't get that far.'

'She works long hours and travels and couldn't cope for a while, especially at work, and the opportunity arose, and it happened. But we have an understanding now,' said Luke gulping some more wine.

I looked at him now I was closer to him, he was handsome with grey eyes and short dark hair and a fit body. But he was at least ten years older than me; I wondered if he could give me the pleasures I needed. Talking with him came easy along with the banter; I was relaxed in his company. It was now starting to get dark outside and then I realized I had forgotten about Lottie. I was slightly light-headed with wine; I was only used to drinking beer.

'Oh, I'm sorry, but I have to go. I have forgotten about my friend Lottie,' I said apologizing to him. 'I don't know where she's gone to, I left her on the beach with some guy, and I haven't seen her since.'

'Why don't you go back to your room to see if she has come back? If she hasn't yet, come back here, and I'll take you out to dinner,' said Luke sounding concerned; God this guy was really something.

'Thanks, I will.' I nodded as I collected my things still wearing his robe, I tottered off back to my villa.

The villa was in darkness as I opened the door, Lottie hadn't come back, but that was how Lottie was if she were enjoying herself, she would stay until the end. Within ten minutes, I had changed into a short alter neck black dress with a pair of slip-on heeled sandals and left with my bag and Luke's robe in hand. I knocked on his door; he answered it nearly straight away as though he was about to go out dressed in light casual trousers and a white shirt. His white shirt brought out his tan, making him look more handsome and sexy.

We walked out of the hotel, walking to a quiet upmarket bar, down one of the side streets. We took our seats as the waiter handed us the menus. Luke asked me if I would like a bottle of wine with our meal. I felt special for the first time, obviously apart from the time Gus had taken me out that evening. It was the second time I had experienced someone taking me out for a romantic meal. We had wine, but I sipped it slowly trying not to drink too much. Our conversation ran smoothly as the evening went on. Luke insisted on paying for the meal as we took a walk on the beach; he took my hand and squeezed it, I felt secure and relaxed in his presence.

I wanted him to pleasure me; I squeezed his hand as we walked along the beach, listening to the sea, rushing back and forth. He stopped and turned to me as I could see him in the shadows shining from the town.

'Liz, would you like me to pleasure you?' asked Luke looking at me with sincerity.

'I was hoping you would,' I whispered as he cupped my face kissing me softly on the lips. I wrapped my arms around him as he started kissing my bare neck; he was making me tingle in the right places and aroused me. His hands ran softly over my body, untying my dress at the top as it dropped to reveal my breasts. With his mouth down to my breasts, he began kissing them gently while cupping them. My nipples hardened instantly, ready for his mouth to take them in. I was starting to come moaning in pleasure, the pleasure that I wanted and missed.

He lifted my dress to expose my black lacy undies, as he pulled the tie at the sides, they dropped to expose me. Luke was going down kissing my body until he was on my clitoris, as he reached there, he gently flicked his tongue, I parted my legs further for him to gain more access to me, my arousal was at boiling point as he inserted his finger inside reaching behind my clitoris and gently rubbing with his thumb. I was moaning loudly with my eyes closed from when he kissed me until he made me come, he kept on going, making me come multiples times, I was in heaven.

We could hear someone coming along the beach; pulling myself together, we set off back to the hotel. He asked me if I would like a drink before going up; I was addicted to him with all the pleasure, I wanted more.

'I better start drinking water,' I muttered as I was feeling slightly fizzy and needed to be sober for my pleasures. Taking a bottle of water, we went up to his room. I consumed nearly half the bottle before I had to go to the bathroom.

Luke was sitting on the sofa, waiting for me to come out. I walked over and sat close to him as he put his arm around me, kissing my neck. I was so aroused I was now about to burst. I turned to straddle over to face him; his hands started to undo my dress, peeling it down to release my breasts as he started kissing me slowly. My nipples hardened once again, god this man was driving me wild, I could feel myself coming as he took my breasts sucking my nipples.

'Oh god, Luke, you're making me come.' I moaned.

He undid my undies from the side to reveal my wetness; I could feel it down my legs. His fingers worked inside me as I came, He then kissed me on the lips, and we exchanged tongues, which made me come again.

After half an hour we made it to the bedroom, the bed was huge. He slowly peeled off the rest of my dress as my undies were left in the other room. I was naked; he was still dressed. I started to undo his shirt as he stood there, watching every move. I peeled off his shirt to expose his tort body; I kissed him gently our tongue mingling fiercely. I went ahead and undid his trousers; they fell to the floor to expose his naked body as he wasn't wearing any underwear.

He had a nice tight butt; I grabbed his butt squeezing him closer to me; I could feel his length hard on me, god I wanted this man inside me. He started kissing me slowly heading down, making me moan in pleasure. Pushing me onto the bed, he parted my legs as he sucked in my wetness gently working his magic fingers and making me come, my wetness kept coming and coming, this man was amazing. He finally came up and entered me, slowly pushing gently in and out gathering speed eventually. I picked up his rhythm, kissing deeply as we both came together. I had never experienced anything like it. The guys always shagged me hard and rough; this was something else to experience.

I lay on the bed sweating in the heat and the pleasures we had endured. There was silence for a few minutes I thought he had fallen asleep as most guys did.

'How are you feeling?' he asked. I rolled over to face him.

'You are amazing, Luke, I had never experienced anything like that before it was wonderful,' I said, kissing him gently on the lips.

'Good, but there's more,' he said, smiling at me.

‘Mm, I can’t wait,’ I said, licking my lips and kissed him again.

‘Luke, would you like me to pleasure you?’ I asked, grinning at him.

‘Yes, if you want to,’ he replied, grinning back at me. I rolled over to straddle him and started kissing him, making my way slowly kissing and licking his tanned skin on every part of his body; he was starting to moan in pleasure. I could feel his length hardening as I was making my way down, and finally, his length was waiting for my attention. I didn’t take him in my mouth as the guys usually want it straight in to get the maximum effect. I started to lick his length kissing it gently until I got to his tip where I took his length in my mouth sucking gently and slowly, his hands on my head going with my rhythm as I sucked harder and quicker and finally made him shot his hot salty liquid.

I swallowed his liquid and finished licking the tip of his length. He pulled me up, kissing me wanting to taste his salty liquid in my mouth as we exchange tongues.

We parted lying on the bed.

'Liz next time you do that, don't swallow, I need to share this with you in your mouth.' I was taken aback as no one had asked me that before.

'Oh, Luke, you are incredible,' I said, wrapping my leg and arm across his body as I snuggled up to him. He brought his arm around as I leaned into his armpit with his hand on my breast. I fell asleep, being relaxed and secure.

When I woke up, Luke was still laid in the same position next to me, and I was relieved he hadn't done a runner. I needed to go to the bathroom and have a drink, I tried not to disturb him, but he was awake, I kissed him as I got up, he held onto me asking where I was going. I was so happy having someone needing me and giving me pleasure.

As I came out from the bathroom Luke wasn't on the bed, he had gone to the chill cabinet for a bottle of chilled water knocking is back emptying the bottle He then handed me a bottle I knocked it back, the pleasure was thirst work, but I loved it. I walked over to the window which looked over onto the sea, the moonlight shining onto the water, making it glisten. Luke came up behind me putting his hands on my shoulders, stroking my body making me tingle with excitement; he started kissing my neck as he cupped my breasts, I started feeling his hardness behind me.

His finger and thumb rubbed my hardening nipples, ready to be sucked; he moved one hand down to enter his fingers inside me, making me moan in pleasure. Turning me around he went down on me making me part my legs as he took my wetness into his mouth sucking my come and with the skill of his fingers and mouth kept making me come over and over again. I leaned back with my eyes closed, holding onto a nearby chair for support. Coming up to kiss me he exchanged my come into my mouth as we exchanged tongues, it was good to taste my own bodily fluid.

I couldn't get enough of him. He massaged my breasts. His length was hard, and I needed to pleasure him, kissing him hard, I worked my way down. He started to moan with pleasure, his length waiting for me as I kissed it up and down licking until his tip started to weep I took his length into my mouth slowly sucking hard, he was moaning as the tension was intense of him wanting to come. I teased him further, and I could feel him wanting to come until he finally did. Holding his liquid in my mouth, I moved up to kiss him, exchanging tongues and kissing with his come.

It was after 8 am, we had been exchanging pleasures all night and needed a shower. I padded off to the bathroom switching on the walk-in shower, while I washed my body and hair I felt a presence enter the shower, Luke had joined me as he ran his hands over my body making me tingle with pleasure, my nipples hardened I was aroused again. With the water running over us, he kissed my mouth a little harder, his hardness filling me up. I wrapped my legs around him to take in his length, holding my weight. I could feel his length so hard.

I whispered to him 'Luke, I am about to come.' and he came with me. We stayed together holding each other as the water ran over us, his length still hard inside me. He put my legs firmly back on the ground as we parted, but his length was still hard. I went down taking it into my mouth sucking it hard to make him come again, within ten minutes he had come, savoring his liquid I gave him a taste of it too.

I needed a change of clothes and had to see if Lottie was in. We arranged to meet at the reception of the hotel for breakfast in about half an hour. I walked back to the villas with a big smile on my face knowing of the pleasures I have had with more to come. Opening to door to the villas I could hear noises coming from the bedroom. I quickly changed into bikini bottoms with shorts and a vest top with flip flops. I could hear grunts and groan with moans of pleasure; hmm Lottie must be ok. I didn't want to disturb her, she was happy. I was just about to leave when the bedroom door opened and out came Cal, one of the guys from the hotel.

'Hi, Liz, why don't you come and join us?' He teased with a smirk. As the bedroom door opened wider, I could see the other three guys we had met when we first came and had our first encounter of two-up with. I wasn't keen on. I could see Lottie was tied to her bed naked she was sucking Lou off while one entered her, and the other watched to wait for their turn. I quickly headed to her bedroom to make sure she was ok being tied to the bed as they abused her. The thumbs-up sign came up as I asked her having her mouth full of cock; the room stank of sex having the top sheet of the bed. I noticed some brown stains. No, she wouldn't, would she? I remembered she liked it up the back passage. These guys were making the most of her knowing that they had taken drugs to keep their sex drive going. But she was happy pleasuring all four of them. We used to talk about our sexual exploits, but I had never heard her talk about being in these situations. I just didn't know her anymore.

As I was leaving the bedroom, Cal caught hold of my arm pushing me back into the bedroom. He grabbed my breast, squeezing them so tight they hurt, I brought my knee up, hitting him between his hard length. He let go releasing his grip on me, giving time for me to escape. I bolted for the door, how did Lottie put up with this? She must have taken something. I quickly ran into the hotel reception to be with Luke; I just hoped he was still waiting for me.

My mind kept wandering to Lottie, and I was hoping that she would be safe with those guys around her.

Something about them did not feel right to me.

Chapter Nine:

Luke was waiting for me, wearing a pair of shorts with a tee-shirt and flip flops, his face lit up when he saw me as I came racing over to him. He put his arm around me, kissing me on the lips and hugging me tightly. We walked out into the brilliant sunshine walking to a bar for breakfast. As we walked hand in hand down the road, I told him about seeing Lottie with the four guys from the hotel and feeling as I didn't know her anymore.

'So, you don't think much to being tied up and anal sex?' he asked.

'Well, not if you don't know them and if you have never experienced it,' I said, thinking what this leading to was.

'I believe Lottie has a great deal of that by the looks of it.' He smirked, giving me the thumbs up.

‘I’m sure she’s taken something. I had to tackle my way out of the bedroom as Cal grabbed hold of me. He pushed me up against the wall with his hand tight on my breasts, but I brought him down on his knees, hitting him between the legs to let go and made a run for it.’ I told him.

‘Hmm, I better be careful and not annoy you,’ he said, laughing.

We arrived at the bar; it was fairly empty as it was early for the people as some were just going home to their hotels from nights partying. Luke insisted on paying the bill; I argued with him and insisted I paid next time. After breakfast, we moved out of the bar walking down the road heading for the beach where we went the evening before.

It was the same beach Lottie, and I had been on, walking further down to cove having discovered the beach where you could strip off. He knew about the cove down there himself, I felt a pang of jealousy, knowing that he may have pleasured others. I didn't ask knowing what happened to Jamie that night.

Kicking off our flip flops and tops, we headed towards the cove paddling in the sea as we walked. We had to squeeze between the rocks to get around the cove on the beach. We found the beach empty; the barman was there waiting to trade. I insisted on buying the drinks and ordered a couple of beers.

'So, what would you like to do?' Luke asked, taking my hand.

'Mm, that's a hard one to answer,' I said with a smirk.

'Well, let's go on further and see what's around the corner,' said Luke, a big grin all over his face. I was already getting aroused knowing what this was leading on to. We stripped off naked as we saw the dunes, the sun warming our bodies as we continued to walk on along the seashore.

Luke grabbed hold of me, tickling me as I tumbled into the water with Luke landing on top of me. He kissed me passionately, taking hold of my breasts and flicked his finger and thumb over my nipple, causing it to harden in pleasure. I could feel every inch of his hard length as he entered me; I was ready to take his full length at once. I lifted my hips in rhythm with his length pushing slowly in and out nearly making me come immediately.

His mouth worked magic on my body as I came; he was still inside me, waiting for me to come again. He took my nipple, sucking it hard as he pushed faster inside me, waiting for the moment for both of us to come together. We laid on the end of the shore as the water brushed over us, cooling us down from the moment of pleasure and the heat of the sun.

I wrapped my arm around his neck, pulling his face toward me, kissing him on the lips; this was arousal in itself.

Leaving my bags and our clothes behind we entered the sea walking up to water up to our waists, Luke dived down, what was he up to? Next moment hands had grabbed my ankles, knocking me off balance; I was under with Luke kissing me as we both came up to feel the sand under my feet. His body pressed close to mine as I could feel his magic fingers working inside me as his kisses slowly skimmed down my neck to my breasts, taking each nipple in turn sucking and teasing with his tongue. I had already come and kept on coming over and over again. I was calling his name as I moaned in ecstasy. He was like a drug; I needed more; he was addictive.

Finding a patch of grass in the shade to lay on, I took the sunscreen from my bag and started to apply it as Luke took over smoothing the cream over my body making me want to come again. He kissed me as he massaged the cream into my breasts, and once he had finished, he started to use his magical fingers pleasuring me. All this while, I couldn't stop moaning with pleasure. All the sex had made me hot and sweaty as though I had done an assault course. I turned over to face Luke as he lay on his back. I took hold of the sunscreen and started to massage the cream on Luke's fit body; his length started to harden, before rubbing the cream in I kissed his body working my way down to his length and balls, kissing his balls up to his length I licked around it until I came to the tip where it was weeping in delight. I licked his tip as he moaned in pleasure, I slowly took him in my mouth, moving up and down over the tip, teasing him as he wanted to come, but I was holding back.

'Liz, you're killing me,' said Luke moaning. I finally took his full length sucking hard, and he came filling my mouth with his salty hot liquid. We held each other tight; it was the place I wanted to be in.

We could see couples coming over to the dunes to make out, so we decided to move and make our way back to the hotel. I needed a drink after a lot of sweating. We bought a couple of beers from the bar in the cove before we headed back, as we approached the narrow entrance we slipped on our shorts and tops before walking any further, but Luke caught hold of me before I changed to put my short on.

He pushed me against the rocks kissing me hard with a lot of tongue action making me come. He wasn't going to get away that easily after which I went down on his length, sucking him hard to bring him on quickly making him moan in pleasure as he came once again.

We stopped at a bar as we headed back, having a well-earned drink and something to eat. By the time we got back to the hotel, it was after 6 pm. I followed Luke to his room; the maid had been cleaning the room and replacing towels in the bathroom and the bedsheets. I needed a change of clothes and a shower, not only that I needed to see if Lottie was still in the villa and that she was ok.

Luke said I could shower in his room, therefore, to fetch some fresh clothes as we would go out later that night for something to eat and drink, I gave him a soft kiss on the lips, and looked into grey eyes licking my lips to tease him. He slapped my backside as I left his room, smiling with pleasure.

I opened the door to the villa; there was silence. I tottered over to Lottie's bedroom to check, the room was tidy with the bed having had fresh sheets, and there were no signs of her apart from her make-up bag being out on the side. Yes, she must be ok. I picked through my clothes. I couldn't decide what I was going to wear, so I picked three outfits out and made my way back to Luke's room.

On entering his room, I saw him stood with a towel around his waist, showing off his deep tan, making him looking handsome and sexy. I wanted to jump on him there and rip off that towel. As I walked in, I turned to face him and said.

'Luke, I need to do this,' but before he asked what? I had dropped my clothes that I had brought with me and peeled off his towel as I started kissing his mouth. I kept going down until I had reached his hard length, I was on my knees holding him by his buttocks as I sucked him hard, giving him pleasure as he moaned and came. I then collected his liquid in my mouth and swallowed. He pulled me up, kissing me as to return the favor then.

We sat on the sofa having a drink from the chiller, we chatted about things in general, but I didn't want to know about the women he had pleasured. Why did he cheat on his wife? I asked myself. I didn't want to spoil my happiness of being with him and having that sort of pleasure, which I knew was not going to last as the holiday would come to an end. It was after 7 pm as I showered and washed my hair, Luke joined me as he pleasured me, making me come multiples times, and I in returned pleasured him.

I walked out of the bathroom naked, drying my hair in the towel; Luke was on the sofa drinking a glass of wine with just a towel around him, his hair slightly damp.

'So, you were going to show me different types of pleasure? I asked.

'Hmm, I will show you, but you will have to trust me,' he said, sounding serious instantly.

I thought about what that could be.

'Ok. I trust you.' I said as I straddled over him, dropping my towel and kissing his lips gently. He gathered me up, lifting to take me to the bedroom and threw me onto the bed; I squealed with excitement, not knowing what he was going to do. He turned me over face down on the bed, his arm rising me up slightly from the back to gain access to enter his magic fingers, massaging me while he started kissing my body all over making me come while I was on my knees.

'Liz, I am going to start, but if you want to stop, tell me.' He whispered as he slowly pushed his finger into my anus; he was gentle as he worked his finger, his other hand started working his fingers inside my vagina, the sensation felt different. Was this the feeling Lottie had in a big way but taking a length and not a finger. As Luke continued manipulating me, I felt the urge to come as I did.

Taking his finger out, he turned me over kissing me exchanging tongues as he entered me with his length pushing slowly waiting for me to come with him.

We lay on the bed for a few seconds, 'so what did you think to it, Liz?' asked Luke.

'Mm different, it was strange to start with but felt good,' I commented.

'How would you feel with having my length in you instead of my finger?' asked Luke, sounding me out.

'Well, I don't know, I'll give it a go, but I will let you know when,' I said, a bit cautious.

'Yeah, just let me know when you're ready,' said Luke sounding sincere.

It was after 10 pm when we went out, down to a bar off one of the side streets for a drink and a sandwich. Luke started to explain why he had cheated, I told him he didn't have to explain, but he did. It was because of his very high sex drive; his wife worked long hours, and her sex drive started to go down, making him look elsewhere. I could see both sides making both sides frustrated with Luke's high sex drive and his wife knowing he needed releasing, but now they had an understanding between them. I felt sadness for them both missing out on this pleasure. Luke had been at the hotel a couple of days before we turned up and was staying a month. I thought who he would be pleasuring when I had gone?

It was gone midnight as we approached a night club where the totes offered us a free drink if we went in. Taking the offer up we took the tickets for a free drink and walked in. The music had stopped, there were girls up on the stage, some half-naked, it was competition time where they asked you a question, and if you answered, incorrectly you had to take off a part of your clothing. I couldn't believe it; Lottie was up there showing her large breasts off as the guys ogled at them.

'Oh my god,' I said, looking at Luke. 'That's Lottie up there showing off her boobs.' Next minute she was naked as she posed her nakedness on stage. She didn't have a care in the world showing off her body. Luke turned to me and asked if I wanted to talk to her; he didn't even ogle her like the other guys were doing.

'No, it's ok. She looks fine; let's get that free drink.' I said, turning and heading for the bar holding Luke's hand as he followed me. I stood at the bar waiting to get served with Luke stood close behind, I could feel his hardness against me, his hand wandered down under my short skirt into my undies as he massaged my sensitive spot. I started to moan as I was about to come when the barman serviced us. I couldn't say anything to him as I was coming. Luke took over and asked for a couple of beers. The club was packed with clubbers, all drunk some naked making out, with others dancing to the music which had started again now the competition had finished.

Luke was grinning as he handed me a beer, I took a quick gulp from the bottle and placed it back on the bar having been surprise pleasured. I turned to face Luke smirking and took him by surprise as I went down, undoing his trousers to release his hard length. I took it in my mouth and sucked him hard in front of the clubbers making him moan in pleasure, and within seconds he had come shooting his hot salty liquid to the back of my throat after which I came up. The clubbers seemed blinded by what we had done. Luke buttoned up his trousers after we had finished kissing both of us grinning at each other. We finished drinking our beers and decided to return to the hotel.

Now I knew Lottie was ok, I was so relaxed being with Luke, but the only problem was I was starting to have feelings for him despite the short period of time we had known each other.

'You're a dark one; I wasn't expecting you, pleasuring me in the club,' said Luke facing me smirking with a raised eyebrow.

'Well you did ask for it making me come

at the bar,' I said, grinning back at him. He kissed me gently on the lips as we carried on walking towards the hotel. We spent the rest of the night pleasuring each other until we both fell asleep in each other arms.

It was after 10 am before we both woke; it was another hot day. I could feel his hardness against my back as he had curled me into his body, having an arm and leg resting over my body. As I moved, I felt his length stir; he was awake as I turned onto my back. Luke slid over me, entering me straight away as he started kissing my neck. With a tongue exchange, my nipples hardened, and arousal below was enough to keep his length gliding slowly back and forth. I lifted my legs parting them wide to gain his full length to the maximum, moaning with pleasure as he waited for me to come, he felt so good inside me I wish we could stay like this forever. Pulling out, he kissed me working his way down to my clitoris drinking in my come and his hot salty liquid. After licking me dry, he made me come again, calling his name in total ecstasy. We both showered together, pleasuring each other before leaving the hotel to have something to eat and drink.

Wearing a vest top and a short skirt with flip flops, we headed off for something to eat and drink. After our meal, I bought a couple of bottles of water to take with us. Instead of going back to the cove we had been the day before, we went to the beach at the front of the hotel; it was a private beach. We had to walk down the cliffs steps zig-zagging; I was hoping there wouldn't be anyone there to share it. Taking nearly 15 minutes to get down, we found the beach empty. There were many secret entrances to hide in, and the sun was at its highest point beating down on us. I didn't know if you could strip off, but what the hell? I still stripped off; Luke did the same as we found the best spot to hide on the beach in case someone came down. We both massaged sun cream on each other while we pleasured each other. As we lay on towels, I was thinking about what Luke had said about the next stage of pleasure, giving me a little in the sight of the finger in my anus with the feeling I would still come, but to take his length, I was prepared to try.

As we laid in the sun taking in the rays for the day, making our tans deeper, I asked Luke about what he had said yesterday about having his full length in my anus.

'Liz, I will be gentle with you, you can stop anytime you want, but I will make you come,' said Luke sounding confident.

'Of course, you haven't disappointed me yet,' I said smirking at him. He grabbed hold of me, spreading my legs apart doggy fashion on all fours. He started stimulating my anus, inserting his finger while his other hand using his magical fingers entered me, my arousal had started despite where his other fingers were. He eased another finger in the tight entrance, but his other magic fingers were relaxing me as the two fingers slid in without feeling any pain. He asked if I was ok.

'Mm just carry on,' I said, holding my breath but in the right way. I could feel his hardness waiting to enter my new entrance. He entered me slowly, easing his length in as his magic fingers stimulated me at the front. I was moaning as he pushed further and further in until his full length was in, the sensation felt good, but as he took hold of my nipple with his finger and thumb and pulled slightly and firmer, I came screaming in pleasure, and he moved inside more quickly waiting to come with me. Within seconds it was over as I held my position on all fours waiting for him to release me, but he stayed there taking both nipples and pulled them as he kissed me at the back of the neck and whispered: 'did you enjoy that?'

I was still moaning in pleasure as he was still moving inside me, pulling firmly on my nipples.

'Oh, Luke, you are so good.' I breathed, as I came again. He backed out as I flopped to the floor being on all fours, he turned me over kissing me hard as he held my breasts pulling my nipples, his kisses ran down my body lifting my legs parting them to gain access to my entrance as he found my clitoris. He played with it with his tongue; I was still wet having come. Drinking in my wetness, he inserted his magic finger in to make me come over and over again. I called his name as I came over and over. He flopped down by the side of me, both of us sweating with the intense pleasuring.

Getting our breaths back we ran into the sea naked; there was no one around, we splashed each other and started to play fight in the water. Luke dived down as I started to swim away, but felt a pull around my waist being dragged down. We were kissing as we came up for air, with my feet firmly on the sand in the sea; Luke hugged me tight cupping my face and kissing me gently on the lips.

‘Are you ok, Liz?’ He stared me in my blue eyes.

‘I have never been so happy,’ I said, kissing him rolling my tongue in his mouth. The water was up to our waists as the waves brushed over us. For over 15 minutes, he kept making me come. I had never been in this situation where a man could stimulate my body so much.

We lay out on towels drying our bodies in the heat of the sun. I wished I could take him home with me, but I knew that was not possible. I wanted to make the most of him giving me my pleasures and experiences I had never had with guys from home. But could Gus give me that despite that we worked for the same company? Should I take a risk and see where it led to? But what did Gus want from me? He was very sincere enjoying the evening he took me out for dinner, conversation with him was smooth, and we kissed. Could it work? I didn’t know. I thought I might speak with Luke about my situation at work with Gus, would he understand my predicament? I thought I would ask that question when it was time to go home. I turned over to lay on my front to even my tanning process, with my arms above my head. I closed my eyes and slowly drifted off to sleep.

I was woken with a start feeling the weight of someone on top of me; my hands were being held together as they enter me hard inside, luckily not my back passage. This wasn't Luke, where the fuck was Luke? He had gone. I tried to struggle, but the weight of the guy on top of me was dead weight, I couldn't move as he hammered hard into me until he shot his lot. After he had finished, I managed to free myself to face him. It was Lou one of the brothers Lottie was blowing being tied to the bed that night.

'You bastard, how dare you?' I shouted.

'You were asking for it laying there. I had to shag it,' he said as if I was just a piece of meat. I was wound up as I got up to punch him, we struggled as I could hear someone coming around the corner of the rocks, but it was his brother Cal. Lou pushed me down as Cal came across. ‘Hold her down for me, Lou while I ride her seeing that she kneed me the other evening.’ I was helpless and naked as Cal drove his hard length inside me, Lou pinned me down pulling my arms back by my wrists, while Cal rode me hard with a hand around my throat as though he was in a rodeo, both brothers must have taken drugs as their eyes were glazed they seemed spaced out. They were both still hard despite having shot their lot, as I endured sex from each brother being pinned down and ridden for over half an hour before they decided they had enough. Their bodily fluids over my body seeping down my legs, I felt dirty, and I had been used treated like a piece of meat.

‘Where the hell was Luke when I needed him?’ I started to cry. How could Lottie put up with these guys?

Getting up after I had stopped crying, I headed for the sea to wash away the unwanted bodily fluids, the sun was going down as the heat of the sun had cooled down. Drying myself, I collected my things and started the climb back up the steps to the villa. I didn't go back to see if Luke was in his room, knowing what had happened with Jamie, it would kill me if he had picked up another woman to pleasure them. Why did he leave me on my own? was I getting too close and was it showing?' I thought.

There was no sign of Luke as I entered the door of the villa; I was surprised to see Lottie.

'Hi, Liz, what have you been up to?' she asked, sounding upbeat and happy. I didn't want to talk about my ordeal I had just had with the twins on the beach.

'Oh, ok,' I said, trying to sound convincing that I was ok. She was getting ready to go out applying her make-up wearing a body-hugging short dress.

'So where are you going tonight,' I asked just to make a conversation.

‘It’s the beach party tonight with plenty of booze and guys,’ she said, licking her lips and sounding excited. ‘Why don’t you come with me?’ she asked.

‘No, I feeling a bit under the weather,’ I said, making an excuse.

‘Oh, that’s a shame, the boys from the hotel are going,’ she said.

‘Yeah, that’s the guys I don’t need to see again.’ I thought. ‘I think I’ve had too much sun,’ I said as I made my way to the bedroom to lay on the bed. Lottie carried on applying her make-up after which I heard her shout out ‘see you later.’

The villa was quiet. I was on a downer, feeling that the rugs had been pulled from under my feet; I turned over on the bed and cried myself to sleep.

Chapter Ten:

I spent the following three days on my own, walking to the beach to sit there and watch people go by and then going back to the hotel to have a stress-releasing swim in the pool. I had to click out of this mood I was in, Luke had gone, which would have happened eventually at the end of the holiday. I didn't see much of Lottie, but when I did, she was always talking about the twins. I didn't want to know, but I had to act normal as I was hurting inside.

Luke had gone, yes it was true, I was falling for him, was that why he had left me? I wouldn't know now. We were over halfway through the holiday, and now I wanted to go home. Everything was falling apart for me; I didn't want to see the twins again as Lottie was, she must be out of her skull being with them.

As my usual drill, after a stress-releasing swim, I pulled myself out of the pool and laid on the sun lounger to dry out. The sun still was radiating heat despite the time of day being 4 pm. I closed my eyes and laid there, topping my tan up in the rays of the sun. As I reached for my drink on the side of the lounger, I heard someone behind me. Without taking any notice, I sipped my drink. I felt a presence standing next to me, but completely ignoring it, I kept my eyes closed.

Then I felt someone kissing me gently on the lips; I recognized that touch instantly. My eyes popped open and met Luke's grey eyes; I wrapped my arms around his neck, pulling him onto me as I kissed him. My mood changed within moments. He was wearing a white shirt with casual trousers, not the beachwear if he had been here all this time.

'Liz I'm sorry left you when you were asleep, I would have been back if it wasn't the message I got from the reception of the hotel, and it didn't cross my mind to leave you a message,' he said deeply apologetic.

I couldn't hold it back. 'Oh, Luke, I've missed you so much,' I said, kissing him all over his face and hugging him tightly, my feelings were showing now.

'Liz, I've missed you too, let's go up to my room, and I'll explain.'

I gathered my things and walked hand in hand with him going up to his room. He opened his door; his room looked as though he hadn't been there, everything was neat and tidy; where the hell had he been? I dropped my things on the floor near the door as I walked in. Closing the door, he took hold of me, kissing me with passion as he wrapped his arms around me, kissing my neck working his way down.

He stripped me naked as he pushed my legs apart to reach my clitoris, his tongue working its magic like his fingers. I lifted my leg on the nearby chair to get the maximum effect, with my hand on his head, gripping his hair as I moaned in pleasure.

'Oh Luke, I've missed this,' I whispered moaning. Coming over and over, my wetness flowed with pleasure as he drank me in and worked his way up to my mouth to give me a taste of my cum. 'God, I've missed you.'

Realizing what I had just said, he scooped me up taking me to the bedroom and pushed me down on the bed. He quickly stripped off as he entered me with his hard length; he was desperate to come.

'Luke, stop,' I said, pushing him to the side. Before he could say anything, I took his length in my mouth and sucked him hard, knowing he was on the verge of coming. Shortly, he was shooting his lot in the back of my mouth, I swallowed it fast, and god I was in love with this man, but could I tell him that?

We lay on the bed sweating, after a few minutes, Luke rolled over to face me, propping his head up with his hand.

'Liz, you know you wanted to know about different sorts of pleasures? Well while you were asleep, I went to get some things for the next stage, but as I went back to the hotel, I had a message waiting for me. It was the hospital; my wife had contracted pneumonia and was in bad condition. I had to go and see her; the next flight was within the hour back to London. I'm sorry Liz, I should have left a message for you at the reception explaining where I had gone, but she is ok now.'

'And here I was thinking the worst that you had had enough of me and found someone else,' I mumbled, reaching over kissing him gently on the lips. I realized what I had said; it was either hit or miss.

'Liz, there's something I need to say,' my face dropped, fearing I was going to be let down gently. 'I have never met anyone like you, you also give me pleasure and know when to use it, and it will soon end when you go home.'

'Hmm I wish I didn't have to,' but I put a brave face on and said, 'Well then, we will have to make the most of the days we have together,' I straddled him kissing him from top to bottom and started to massage his length and balls with my mouth making him hard. He pulled me up, turning me over; I struggled as I tried to fight him, wanting to please him again. We tussled on the bed to gain dominance with me losing the fight as he entered me, cupping my breasts and taking my hard in his mouth. He massaged my breasts, waiting for me to come so we could come together.

I needed some clothes to change into, so I nipped out to the villa to collect a few things. I could hear Lottie as

I opened the door quietly, her bedroom door was open. I couldn't believe want I was seeing; she must be taking drugs as the four guys from the hotel had her tied spread-eagled out on the bed, naked. They were taking it in turns entering her in every orifice while the others waited their turn pummeling at her body, especially her large breasts.

I tried to be as quiet as possible, quickly gathering what I came in for laying my hands on any clean clothes without being spotted by one of the guys. I managed to find what I wanted and turned heading for the door, but I caught the chair leg with my foot making it scrape across the floor. Cal looked across and saw me, making a leap for the door. I ran holding onto my clothes panic within me as I was lucky enough to have had left the door open to the villa, making a quick exit. I had escaped, Cal made no effort to chase me, and I was relieved as I walked up to Luke's room to change.

Luke answered the door naked. 'How did you know it was going to be me?' I asked.

'Well, I was asking for room service,' he said grinning. Placing my clothes on the side, he grabbed hold of me, bending me backwards and kissing me passionately on the lips. His kisses seemed more than just pleasure, it was something else, was I imagining this or was I reading into that I wanted to?

I pulled him down onto the floor; he stripped me naked as he entered me, 'Luke don't wait for me, fuck me hard, I need you to do this for me.' I whispered. He did, it felt different from others that had fucked me hard, and this had meaning while the other didn't. He came and was going down, but I stopped him pushing him away as I went down to clean him up and to pleasure his balls and length taking my time to bring his length back to hardness. I needed to pleasure him as he was pleasuring me. I knew I was falling in love with him.

We showered together, Luke pleasuring me multiples times before we exited the room to have an evening meal together.

It was after 8 pm as we entered the bar taking a seat at the back of the room. It was romantic; Luke ordered a bottle of wine while we pondered over the menu. I watched him as he scanned the menu; he was looking handsome in his light blue shirt opened at the neck showing his tan. I then looked at his grey eyes, were they going to tell me anything? I could have climbed over the table and devoured him and fucked him senseless, giving him his pleasure instead of mine.

We chatted while we ate, he asked me about the flatmates I lived with. I told him about Emma leaving us to work in London as she had got a promotion and had to move. I described her with the piercing and where they were on her and said I wouldn't mind having one in my clitoris as she had. Luke raised an eyebrow as I said it and then asked me what I did for a living. I explained that I had two jobs only because all my friends had partners and I didn't, as I had explained when I first met him. I told him where I worked at a bar and that we were asked to wear these sexy uniforms to bring more customers in. And that I had only been doing it a couple of weeks before I told Jerry I was going on holiday and he wasn't very happy about it as the uniform had made a big difference to his takings.

'Mm,' he said 'I wouldn't mind seeing you in that.' he licked his lips.

'Well, you'll have to come over and see me in action,' I said, sounding sexy and wishful.

'Yeah, so where is this place?' he asked.

'It's called Seventh Heaven; it's in the city centre of Manchester,' I said, moving my tongue across my top lip and waggling it at him. He looked at me, taking my hand as his fingers circled my palm; he was arousing me with his touch.

'Luke, we have to go.' I said, looking into his eyes as I got up from my seat leaning over and whispered, 'I need to please you hard.' He took my hand, pulling me towards him and kissing me passionately on the lips.

'Come on, let's go.' He said as he left some notes on the table.

We were back in his room by 10.30 pm stripping off and eating each other. First, he pleasured me after which I said I needed him to fuck me hard to please him. After an exhausting hour, we lay sweating and catching our breath after vigorous sex. As we laid there, Luke turned over and asked if I wanted the next stage of pleasure. Wow, could this get any better? I thought.

'I'm waiting,' I said as I turned to face him looking into his grey eyes with a smirk.

'You trust me, don't you?' he asked, sounding serious.

What had he in mind? I wondered.

'Of course, I do,' I said, licking my lips to tease him. He kissed me quickly as he jumped up from the bed heading towards the chest of drawers near the window.

I laid waiting in anticipation of what he was going to do; he told me to close my eyes. I could hear him unwrapping something, padding across and kneeling on the bed.

'You still trust me, don't you, Liz?' he asked just double checking before he started.

'Yes, I trust you with my life,' I said, licking my lips teasing him with my eyes still closed. I could feel him buckling a strap on my wrists as he moved them into the position, tying them to the headboard and again with my ankles to the bottom of the bed. He had me spread eagle naked on the bed and vulnerable. This was how I had seen Lottie with the four guys from the hotel banging the hell out of her. The difference was, she did not know the guys who were just totally abusing her body, but not realizing it as she was enjoying it. Luke noticed a change in my breathing and asked me if I was ok.

'Umm-hmm I think so,' I said, sounding not very confident.

'Liz, open your eyes and look at me. I can stop if you want me to and release you,' said Luke. As I opened my eyes, Luke kissed me gently on the lips; 'You're safe with me.'

'I know I am; it's just I've seen Lottie in our villa with those four guys. They had tied her up and were abusing her, being rough. I think she had taken something to endure what I saw.' I said, being a little dramatic.

'Yes, I had noticed they are a bit out of hand, and it would put it past them taking something, and I should say your friend would possibly have as well to endure their sexual exploits,' said Luke sounding serious.

'Luke, I need you to take me. I'm yours to please.' I said, stretching to kiss him. He straddled his naked body over me, kissing me passionately on the lips as he slowly made his way down, kissing and licking every part of my body. My arousal was quick as my nipples were hard from his mouth. He parted my labia to access my clitoris, I had already come and was coming again, I came as his thumb rubbed the top drinking in my wetness, I couldn't stop moaning with pleasure calling his name. I wanted to hold him but I couldn't; God I thought Lottie was missing out on what pleasure could be for her. His magic fingers entered me, causing me to come again; he was killing me with pleasure, working his way up slowly kissing my body until he reached my lips, giving me a meaningful, passionate kiss as though he was falling for me, too. I was desperate to hold him and pleasure him. Luke bent over the side of the bed as I heard him taking something out of a bag. It looked like a chain with clamps.

'Liz, tell me to stop if you want me to.' He instructed as he applied the clamps to my hard nipples I winced a little, he stopped.

'No, don't stop,' I said the feeling was starting to harden my nipples further and making me wet; it was arousing me further even without his touch. He lifted the chain to put a little tension making the clamps pull on my nipples, it felt so good as I moaned asking him to pull the tension more, it was so intense I soon came. He kissed me exchanging tongues and straddled over me.

'Luke, I want you inside me. Fuck me hard and pull those chains harder.' I said in a dominant voice, I was experiencing a new sensation and would come with him as he pushed hard inside me. His juices and mine mixed together. He inserted his fingers and gradually fisted me inside as he pulled on the chains; it was like turning a switch on, the sensation making me explode.

Luke started to massage our fluids on my body and entered my anus, making me flinch a little.

'Are you ok, Liz?' he asked.

'Yes, yes,' I said, needing him to carry on.

'Liz, I'm going to untie you and turn you around but only tying your hands again,' said Luke. As he undid my shackles, I wanted to jump on him, but he soon had me turned over and shackled again, leaving my ankles free. I was on my knees with my hands now still tied. The clamps were still on my nipples swaying beneath me as I was kneeling waiting for him to enter me from behind. His fingers lubricated my behind, waiting for him to enter me slowly. As he started, I held my breath, his fingers taking me from the front as he slowly pushed his way in, working his length and his fingers together. Finally, he took hold of the chain and pulled, working all three together sending tingles I had never experienced before.

He made me come as I moaned in pleasure, calling his name. 'Push harder,' I demanded him, who was still pulling on the chains as he came. I was breathing heavily and sweating with the excision. For a few seconds, we stayed locked together after which he untied my shackles taking hold of me kissing so passionately.

We showered together, cleaning ourselves of bodily fluids as there was plenty of it. He washed my body all over and took the opportunity to keep pleasuring me. Taking the sponge off him, I washed his body from top to bottom, and while I was down there, taking his length and sucking him hard to give him his pleasure in return.

It was nearly 3 am before we were back on the bed. We chatted about my insight of a little bondage and the clamps. The clamps were a new experience for me, sending me to the next level of pleasure. He asked me about the job I did, working part-time behind the bar and wearing the uniform as customers being a handful when drunk. I said I could handle it and would nip it in the bud before it grew out of control. He kissed me, saying I was beautiful and why no one had scooped me up for themselves.

'I guess I must say the wrong things and they run a mile, but they only want sex with me, they don't want to take it any further and have a relationship,' I said, sounding disappointed.

'Well they don't know what they're missing out on,' said Luke as he kissed me softly and then so passionately, I was definitely falling for him.

For the rest of the days that were left of my holiday, I moved into his room, feeling safer despite leaving Lottie with the four guys from the hotel. She seemed to know what she was doing and was quite happy with it. We dined out, walked on the beach but spent a larger part of our time in his room pleasuring each other to the maximum limit, as I slowly was falling in love with him. I was dreading the day I was to return home back to normality.

On the very last night before I was due to go home, we did everything possible for each other that would send us to heaven and back. We wrestled with each other trying to take control of who was pleasuring who. After he came, I would keep on bringing him up sucking and licking him, which didn't take long. It was a good thing that he had a very high sex drive. I needed to drink as much as possible from him knowing I would not see him again. He said nothing about wanting to see me again, which was killing me as I loved him, but I didn't push it.

The morning had arrived; that would put an end to my ecstasy, leaving behind a man I had started to love. Lottie was waiting in the hotel reception with her bags wearing a white hugging dress with enough cleavage showing off her tanned assets, looking well considering she had more sex in two weeks than she had in one year. Luke followed me down to the reception carrying my suitcase. We all ventured out as the coach had turned up to take us to the airport; my eyes started to well up as a tear escaped from the corner of my eye. I quickly tried to take the moisture away from my eyes, running my finger across my eyes without Luke noticing.

The coach driver started to put our cases into the baggage rack inside the side of the coach. Lottie disappeared onto the coach to find a good position as it was empty. I was left with Luke, so I hugged him as the driver was now waiting for me to get on board for the airport.

'Luke, you are the most gentle, understanding and lovable person I have ever met and will always remember you for showing me the pleasures I always missed.'

He kissed me passionately as we parted; tears were now showing as they ran down my cheeks. The coach driver was now getting impatient as time was getting on. With one last kiss, I whispered in his ear telling him that I loved him before turning running to get onto the coach. Seating down with Lottie the coach pulled away, and I burst into tears knowing I wouldn't see Luke again.

As we travelled together, Lottie seemed like a stranger. I felt as though I didn't know her anymore, knowing what she had been doing while on holiday with the four guys from the hotel using her. The journey to the airport was silent. She didn't even ask me about Luke, so I didn't offer any information; I didn't want to talk about it. Lottie slept on the plane home as I was thinking of losing the love of my love knowing I would never see him again.

My heart was broken. I had never felt like this before over a guy. The only thing I knew about him was that he still loved his wife despite being separated and I found out soon after it was to release him from his very high sex drive not holding him back for his pleasures.

Monday morning had come around it was hard to get into the rhythm of work after having two weeks off. I was commented on my tan and was teased if I had any white bits. While scrolling through all my emails for two weeks and picking out the most important one to deal with, I needed a coffee.

I was thinking of Luke while I boiled the kettle, and heard someone coming in behind me.

'Hi Liz, you are looking well, you must have had a good holiday,' said Matt standing next to me with an empty mug in his hand, also waiting for the kettle to boil.

‘Mm, I did thanks,’ I replied, still dreaming of Luke pleasuring me.

‘Did you see the list I’ve sent everyone about the clearance stock we need to push?’ said Matt now back in working mode.

‘Yeah, I see you still have stocks left over from two weeks ago.’ I sighed.

‘Well, what do you expect? I didn’t have my number one girl here, did I?’ said Matt grinning at me.

‘Yeah, you can stop that flannel,’ I said, pouring the boiling water in my mug and headed out to the sales office.

The day soon went as I got back into the swing of things; jovial banter being thrown across the office as we worked making the end of the day to come around to 5 pm. I managed to finish on time to leave with the others as we still bantered heading for the door. Since we had come back from the holiday, Lottie seemed quiet and tried to avoid me by going out. The flat was silent as I opened the door. I decided to eat out and see how Jerry was doing at the bar despite it being a Monday night. I changed into something comfortable, a pair of jeans and a tee-shirt combined with a pair of pumps, the weather was still warm but not as hot the two weeks we were away. I was missing Luke's touch as a stray tear escaped my eye corner, 'for fuck sake, Liz, get a grip I said to myself.' I wasn't going to see him again, and I should as well just get on with my life. But it was like having had a diamond, and now you were left with glass.

Chapter Eleven:

It was nearly 6.30 pm when I arrived at the bar; Jerry was behind the bar bottling up as I walked in.

'Hi.' I waved cheerfully. Jerry turned around and stood up,

'Oh, Liz, I'm so glad you're back. Everyone has missed you, the customers have been asking where you were,' said Jerry, pleased to see me. 'You look so well with that tan, any white bits left?' he asked winking at me.

'No cooked all over,' I smirked at him. 'Did you find anyone while I was away?' I asked.

'Well, not really. One of the waitresses covered but wouldn't wear the uniform. I must say the two weeks you were off the takings were down.' Jerry sounded disappointed.

'Mm, I must be doing something right,' I said, raising an eyebrow and smirking.

'You have a way with the guys, I don't know why you're not spoken for,' said Jerry.

'Well, I haven't found the right one yet.' I smiled, thinking of Luke who would never be mine.

'So, what brings you here?' asked Jerry.

'No one is in, and I thought I would eat out, so what's on the menu tonight?' I asked.

'Just the usual for a Monday,' replied Jerry.

I went through to the kitchen. Pete was preparing sandwiches for a birthday party which were supposed to be collected shortly; it was for one of the elderlies in a caring home as a surprise. Pete made a couple of sandwiches for me as I sat and chatted to him while he prepared them.

'Jerry wasn't pleased with the taking while you were away, you certainly make a difference. I don't know what you say to them,' said Pete giving me a look.

'You can stop looking at me like that Pete,' I said, lapping him on the arm as I got up and headed out to the bar area.

Standing at the bar was a lone guy, leaning against the bar with a pint in his hand. I recognized him it was Jamie. I could have punched him seeing him with that woman, and for telling that guy in the band I did a good blow job, but I had to get over Luke. Walking over to him, I put my hand on his shoulder.

'Now then stranger what you are doing here?' I said, sounding as nothing had happened. Jamie lifted his head, and as soon as he saw me, he snaked his arms around my waist, drawing me into his warm body. The touch of a man felt good.

'Liz, where have you been? I haven't seen you for two weeks,' he asked as though I was his property.

'I've been on holiday, away. I thought you had finished working around here.' I said with a little sarcasm.

'We started another job nearby, and I was looking for you to explain about the woman I was with, she was my wife, we are separated, but we lead our own lives,' he said as he kissed me.

Well, that taught me one thing; when you see the worst, don't make your conclusion on the matter, I had got it wrong. I shrugged off his comments as I kissed his lips, so different to Luke's. I had to stop comparing guys with Luke.

'So, what are you up to tonight?' asked Jamie grinning at me.

'Nothing,' I said.

'Come on, then let's get out of here back to my place,' said Jamie.

'Do I resist temptation or resistance is futile? I asked myself. It was the latter, as we both walked out of the bar together. His flat was empty. I wondered if he had now had the place to himself. We kissed as he pulled my top off, revealing my black lacy bra and my tanned body. After unhooking the back as my breasts fell into his hands, he squeezed them, his hands slightly rough in comparison with Luke's. Pushing me onto the bed, he unbuttoned my jeans, pulling them off to reveal my skimpy undies, I could see his length hard beneath his jeans.

'Wow, you have no white bits. I thought I would find some,' said Jamie as he slid off my undies, making me naked in front of him. He released his beast and thrust it inside me. He was like a piston I could feel his ring inside me, and I was slowly coming, but he spoilt it by coming himself as he flopped on top of me. I sighed; it was going to be back to the same old thing; I wasn't going to get any pleasure. Jamie rolled overlaying there, sod this, I wished I was with Luke, it didn't feel right. Then I dressed and was out of the door in a flash. I had made a mistake again; these guys were just having sex, using my body for their pleasure and not mine.

I walked home disappointed; it was getting on for 9 pm. I wondered if Lottie would be home? We hadn't spoken about the holiday or spoken much in general since we had come back. I was sure she was trying to avoid me. I took the long route home, taking my time getting back to the flat around 10 pm.

The light was on that would mean Lottie would be home. 'Hmm, here it goes.' I braced myself as I opened the door. I walked into the living room where Lottie was on the sofa watching the TV.

'Hi, Liz, where have you been tonight?' asked Lottie a little nervously.

'Oh, went to see Jerry see how he got on while I was away and while I was there Jamie came in, so we went back to his place,' I said not sounding excited about it.

'Oh, I thought he was the guy you saw with another woman when you went around to his place off speck,' said Lottie.

'Yeah, he said he had been looking for me to explain, saying it was his wife. They are separated but go their own way.' I said flatly.

'Hmm, do you believe him? She asked.

'I don't know any more, Lottie, I know what I need now but whether I'll find it or not I don't know.' I sighed heavily, slumping on the sofa with Lottie.

'You're in love, aren't you, Liz?' asked Lottie, sounding sympathetic.

‘I left him in Corfu, and I will never see him again, but it was an experience,’ I said sobbing lightly, a tear rolling down from the corner of my eye. Lottie moved over to hug me; it was the first time since we had come home that we started a normal conversation. It all came flooding out; I felt my heart had broken. Soaking Lottie’s blouse with my tears and blabbering under my tears and sobs, I told her everything. Lottie reached for the tissues on the coffee table, handing me the box; I grabbed a handful plugging my nose from the snot coming out.

It was nearly half an hour before I could not cry any more, so I started to pull myself together. I told Lottie I had been with Jamie back to his flat where he used me for his own needs after he had finished, I left him.

’It was like going back to Groundhog Day; I don’t want it anymore Lottie. I need someone to love and pleas me.’ I said, sounding as though I was desperate.

'You will find someone, Liz when you least expect it,' said Lottie in a calming way.

'Yeah, I suppose you are right Lottie.' We chatted about the first day back to work and eventually the holiday with the four guys we first met at the hotel. Lottie admitted about taking drugs with the guys as it made her feel good. The guys tying her up, using her body for their pleasure as they spread their bodily fluids in and over her and pummeled her breasts. She said that it gave her a feeling of power and a high having four guys using her body as they wanted. I didn't understand why she had done it, but I didn't ask her any further, it was her life to live the way she wanted.

Alice was due to move in on Sunday, Emma had left the room clean and tidy before she moved out, and so we had nothing to do on that side. The rest of the week flew by having got back into the swing of things at work, picking up on the stock clearance list and pushing hard to sell to customers as they placed their regular orders for the week. By Friday before my shift ended, I had sold most of the clearance stock plus the ones from two weeks I was off. I was pleased with myself for meeting my goal, as I was aiming for as now to concentrate on my job just to get out of the holiday mood.

Thursday evening soon came around; I left the flat by 6.30 pm to be at the bar for 7 pm. Jerry was fixing one of the taps on the beer pumps as I walked in.

'Hi, Jerry,' I shouted across, heading to the back room. Jerry didn't acknowledge me, but I could hear him swearing at the pumps as he was trying to fix them. Oops, he won't be in a perfect mood if he'd got problems with the pumps. Taking off my jacket and hanging it with my bag, I walked out of the backroom to set the tables and chairs in the bar area after which I placed the beer mats on the tables.

There was music playing in the background sounding a little dull, so I decided to turn the tempo up a few notches with a bit of Bon Jovi and Kiss, singing and dancing around the bar as I tided around. After Jerry had finished fixing the pumps, I had to clean his mess up; uh typical guy.

Hearing the loud rock music blaring out from the pub, customers were starting to come in thinking that something was going on, only to see me dancing behind the bar singing along with the music. Still, they stayed even for the entertainment I was giving them. I was in a happy mood, forgetting what I had left in Corfu and was just living in the moment. Sarah, Jody and I selected the songs to be played mainly to lift the atmosphere in the bar as we sang in unison and danced behind the bar as we enjoyed the banter and the music.

By 10 pm the bar was full, having enough room to mill amongst the customers as I collected the empty glasses with some of the guys dancing with me as they squeezed my butt, it was expected to be part of the job.

11.30 pm had soon come around, which was time for me to go while Sarah and Jody cleaned and tidied up being full-time bar staff. As soon as I was out of the door, Jamie grabbed hold of my waist from the back making me jump, I turned around and was about to throw a punch when I realized who it was.

'You were lucky I didn't give you a left hook,' I said slightly nervous from the fright.

'Sorry Liz, I didn't mean to frighten you,' said Jamie being apologetic.

'Hmm, so what are you up to?' I asked as I started walking towards home.

'I've been waiting for you to finish work,' said Jamie hugging me tight as we walked.

‘Oh, what for?’ I asked, testing my theory of what guys wanted.

‘Fancy coming back to my place?’ asked Jamie, sounding upbeat.

‘No, I’m going home,’ I said bluntly with no hesitation.

‘Oh, come on, Liz, you’re always up for it,’ said Jamie trying to convince me.

‘Sorry Jamie things have changed,’ I said, pulling away from him.

‘Another time maybe then,’ said Jamie as I left him standing on his own.

‘Yeah, whatever.’ I carried on walking towards home.

It was Friday morning the weather was starting to turn as summer had begun to turn into autumn, there was a slight chill in the air as I walked to work. I was in early having not read through all my emails from the day before which needed answering urgently. At least I would have some peace and quiet being on my own without being disturbed, knowing it could get rather hectic with the phones ringing non-stop and the occasional round of banter going around the office.

As 8.30 am approached, staff started trickling in, firstly switching on their computers and heading off to the staff kitchen for coffee to wake themselves up for the morning's rally with the phones. Matt was the first before the rest followed.

'Liz, can you come into my office when the others are in? I need to speak to you in confidence,' said Matt touching my shoulder as he walked off to his office.

'What the hell have I done now?' I thought he hardly spoke to me in general. It must be something important, or I was in for my P45.

I went off to make coffee when everyone was in and disappeared into Matt's office. I knocked on his door which was slightly ajar, pushing it open Matt motioned for me to come in and closed the door.

'Sit down, Liz, there's nothing to worry about,' said Matt smiling at me. I sat down, placing my mug of coffee on his desk and waited for him to speak. 'Liz, this is strictly between you and me ok?' he said in a severe manner.

'Yes, of course,' I said, not knowing what he was going to say.

'Well, I am leaving and moving overseas to another branch of the company, which means my job will be vacant. I have been asked higher up if you would apply for the job when it's advertised? Because you are very good with the customers and could sell sand to the Arabs. It has been noticed that you are the best candidate in the sales team boosting the company's profits and clearing old stocks out.' I gulped coffee, not knowing what to say.

'Oh, I wasn't expecting this,' I said, sounding gobsmacked that the company had appreciated me by more or less offering me Matt's job as Sales Manager.

'Your pay would increase enormously,' said Matt smiling at me. I had to process this more thinking of the responsibilities I would have to take on.

'Do I want it?' I asked myself. I left Matt's office without the sales team noticing that I had been in. I sat at my desk with my coffee which was now nearly cold. After an hour I had to have another coffee and to go to the bathroom thinking about Matt's job as Sales Manager. I thought of Emma; she had her promotion moving to London, which she was aiming for. I wasn't aiming anywhere only doing my job to the best of my ability. As the day went on, I was inundated with customers needing to speak to me, having two phone calls to make before going home. It was already after 5 pm as the rest of the staff had gone with it being a Friday; Matt was the last to leave asking me if I was ok with my calls.

'Yes, thanks. I've only got a couple more calls to make before I go.' I said, picking the phone and dialling the number. Matt patted me on the shoulder as he left. He had never done that before touching me on my shoulder; I always thought he was too them and us being standoffish.

It was nearly 6 pm as I headed to the kitchen with my mug to wash. I rushed for the door as the door hit back at me as someone was coming into the staff kitchen. The door hit my head, knocking me back slightly as I focused on the person coming in from the other side. It was Gus.

'Liz, I'm so sorry. I didn't think anyone would be in here at this time of the day,' said Gus holding to steady me with his arm around my waist.

'Nor was I, but I had a couple of customers to phone urgently before I left,' I said slightly flustered as I gazed into his blue eyes.

'Are you sure you're ok?' said Gus sounding concerned with the bump I just had.

'Yes, thanks I'm ok, but it's making me late for the bar,' I said as I tore away my eyes from his and composed myself to exit out of the door.

'Sure. I may see you later,' said Gus trying to get my attention, but I was gone rushing back home to have a quick shower before heading to the bar for 7 pm.

It was times like this when I needed my car, but after changing my job, I didn't need it, not only that it was a good excuse not to meet anyone. Also, it would cost me money only to be used probably once a month if that. Lottie gave me a quick squirt of perfume a client of hers had given her. It smelt gorgeous leaving a lingering smell as I walked back through into the bar.

'You smell nice, Liz,' said Jerry sniffing the air as I walked past him.

'Thanks, it's something that Lottie was given from a client of hers,' I told him as I started moving the tables and chairs ready for the evening.

'Would you mind asking her if I could purchase some from her? My wife would love it,' said Jerry sniffing the air again.

'Yeah I'll ask her, but I can't promise anything.' 8 pm had soon come around, and we had to change to our sexy outfits as Jerry said, dress to impress the customers and flaunt your assets.

Jerry had no live band on tonight, so the three of us girls decided to set the playlist of music to liven the bar and to get in the mood as if we were having a party.

'Hey, what choices do you want for the playlist?' I asked Jody and Sarah.

'We can have the same as last night if you want, Liz,' said Jody being happy with the list we had played last night.

'I was thinking about adding a few odd ones in considering we here later today.'

'I'm sure you can think of something, Liz,' said Jody as she went off to serve a customer. Seeing that the two girls could look after the bar, I went to flick through various sounds of music to add to the playlist. Mm, these might do the trick. Adding to the playlist; Don't cha by the Pussycat Dolls, Wannabe by The Spice Girls, Lumbada by Kaoma, Livin La Vida Loca by Ricky Martin, I Love Rock 'n' Roll and I Hate Myself for Loving You by Joan Jett. I thought when the Lumbada played I would go out to collect the empty glasses and give some of the guys a close contact with me dancing the Lumbada. I was grinning to myself as I set the tracks up and pressed play for the list to start, turning up the volume.

As the music blared out, the bar started to get busy, bringing in the guy's in, listening to rock music. All three of us were being ogled at as the guys waited to be served, undressing us with their eyes, as we walked from serving each customer. I started to tease them walking and touching myself provocatively, winding them up. Jody and Sarah noticed what I was doing and started to do it, too. Some of the guys got carried away as they tried to grab us, but with them being hardly able to stand up, their reactions were slow.

Jerry came through from helping out in the kitchen, 'why have you changed my playlist?' asked Jerry.

'Well, you never said anything last night, anyway us girls run this bar and the music, so bugger off,' I said as I walked off slapping my hand on my butt while going over to serve a customer.

As soon as I had finished serving, the music changed to the Lumbada. I quickly told Jody and Sarah I was going to collect empties as I lifted the bar top into the bar. I noticed a group of good-looking guys on the other side of the room, mm let's do some teasing, I thought. They saw me coming over as they started to jostle for position to speak to me, but I started the conversation first.

'Come on, which one of you is going to Lumbada with me?' a tall, dark hair guy grabbed me, taking me around the waist holding me tight as we started to sway to the music with our hips to the rhythm of the music, 'Hmm you've done this before.' I nodded appreciatively, teasing him. Our hips and closeness went in rhythm to the music as the customers looked on; we were giving them a bit of entertainment. He was good; I wondered what he was like in bed, feeling his length hard against my body, as he kept a tight hold of me throughout the song.

After the song finished his mates whistled and cheered. He kept hold of me kissing me on the lips softly; it made me tingle and started to arouse me. ‘You’re a good mover,’ he whispered in my ear as he hugged me.

‘Yeah, I’m.’ I gave him a soft kiss before I said I needed to start collecting the empties. As he released me, I started walking around the bar collecting empties where I was getting hugged, slapped on the butt, kissed and groped from all sides, but underneath I loved it. I suppose it was the attention I was getting and a bit of an exhibitionist.

Gus had been watching me as I approached the bar with a handful of empty glasses.

‘Hello, how long have you been in?’ I asked, surprised to see him.

‘Mm about five minutes, long enough to see you, doing the Lumbada with that guy,’ he said, sounding a little jealous.

‘Oh, not long then.’ I smiled, trying to string off his comment. Nipping in behind the bar, I cleared the empty glasses putting them in the washer. I switched the machine on now it was full.

‘Have you had your break yet, Liz?’ he asked as though he had something to say.

‘No, but I’m due one, I’ll just let the girls know, and I’ll be with you in a minute.’ After informing the girls, I took Gus to the back room, where it was quieter and had somewhere to sit.

‘So, what are you up to?’ I asked curiously as he was on his own.

‘I’ve come to see you,’ he said, looking into my eyes. His piercing blue eyes were telling me to go to bed with him, but I had to focus; he was a work colleague. ‘You left in a rush, and I didn’t have a chance to ask you out to dinner again,’ he said anxiously, hoping I would say yes.

‘Aw, Gus I don’t want you spending your money on me. I’m not worth it.’ I said, trying to turn him down gently.

‘Liz, you are to me, please its only dinner we can go to a little pub on the outskirts of the city if you want.’

‘Gus you are such a nice guy if you weren’t a work colleague I would jump at the chance.’ I kissed him softly on the lips, feeling a tingle running through my body, wow there was some sort of connection there, and I think he felt it too.

‘Oh god Gus, you are so irresistible, but we need to take this slowly and make sure no one knows at work,’ I said, giving in. His face lit up, with a huge grin, he kissed me and said thank you.

'I need to get back to work now,' I said, feeling that he wanted to say something else.

'I'll pick you up at 7 pm, but it will have to be the first Tuesday of the month as I am away then, is that ok with you?' asked Gus sounding me out.

'Yes, ok.' I got up needing to go back to work.

I went back to work, not seeing Gus for the rest of the night; he must have left. Was it because he didn't like seeing me teasing the guys, or was it something else? I supposed time would tell. It was nearly 2 am as the bar was thinning out. I noticed the guy I had danced with was still there with his group, being noisy and jovial with each other.

I wondered seeing that if we were serving the odd customer, I went to the playlist and over rid the songs until I got to the Lumbada and pressed play. I stepped out to collect empty glasses around the room now the bar was emptying. As I walked towards them pretending it was just part of my job they saw me, as the same guy jumped up to grab me around the waist hugging me tight as our hips moved with the rhythm of the music. His hands slid down to my butt squeezing, as I could feel his hardness against me bursting to enter me with his tight jeans and his toned body. He kept whispering in my ear and nibbling my ear lobe; he was arousing me fast.

'What time do you finish?' he asked.

'About 3 am,' I said, waiting for him to answer.

'Can't you leave any earlier?' he asked, pushing his luck.

'No, I need to finish tidying up before everyone has gone,' I said, I wasn't giving in as I would have done before making myself looking easy. As the music finished, he kissed me, and I struggled free to start collecting the rest of the empty glasses.

It was 3 am before I left, Jerry was pleased with the night takings now that I was back behind the bar earning a pleasant bonus. As I stepped outside into the early hours of the chilly morning, the streets were quiet; it only took me less than half an hour to walk home at a quick walking pace. But as I started to stride out, a figure stepped out in front; it startled me as I took a deep breath in. It was Jamie.

'Jamie, don't do that, you startled me.' I kept on walking fast, needing to get home.

'Liz, hold on a minute I need to talk to you,' said Jamie holding onto my arm as he pulled me backstopping me in my tracks.

'What do you want?' I said, sounding abrupt.

'Liz, I saw you, dancing with that guy, I was a little envious seeing him touching you and being so close, come with me I need you Liz.' he started to plead with me.

'No, Jamie,' I said, holding my ground. 'I'm going home.' and started walking off.

Jamie grabbed hold of my wrist as he twisted it around pushing my arm behind my back, his body pressing against mine. I could feel his length beneath his jeans he was bursting, wanting a release, but it wasn't going to be me anymore. He pushed me against the wall as he tried to kiss me, his kiss hard and forced; his hand grabbed my breast, squeezing them hard as he pushed me tighter to the wall.

He was desperate; it wasn't the Jamie I once knew. I found my strength as I brought my knee up to his length, making him release his grip, giving me enough time to free myself and run. Jamie was on his knees, calling me all the names under the sun as his hands nursed his manhood from the pain I had given him. I kept on running until I got home and was relieved as I opened the flat door, knowing that I was safe.

Chapter Twelve:

I could hear Lottie banging about in the kitchen, waking me up from a deep sleep. I pulled my pillow over my head to dim the noise, but it made no difference, so I decided to get up knowing that I wasn't going to get any more sleep. Slipping my robe on, I padded my way through to the kitchen.

'Lottie, what the fuck are you doing?' I asked, looking rough and sounding half asleep.

'Oh, sorry, Liz, I thought, I would give the kitchen a good clean seeing that Alice is moving in tomorrow.'

'I don't know why you're bothering,' I said, turning around to flick on the kettle to make coffee.

'Well, you know what? Some people are fussy about the cleanliness of a kitchen,' said Lottie as she pulled on opened packs of various things, we had tried to cook during the year we had been together, but it hadn't worked out, and they were pushed to the back of the cupboard never to be seen again until now.

'I thought we got rid of those.' I wrinkled my nose, picking one of the open packs and thinking of the disaster of the evening when we had cooked that meal and had to go out to get a takeaway. I went into the living room with my coffee, leaving Lottie to finish off cleaning in the kitchen.

I sat on the sofa switching the TV on but only to think about Jamie being so pushy and demanding. He was showing another side to him, and I was glad I didn't go with him knowing that he wanted to use my body and not me as a person. I just hoped he wasn't waiting for me tonight when I left work at the same time. This was the time I could have used my car, but sold it soon after when I changed my job. I thought I could get a taxi, but at that time in the morning, they charged a fortune which would make working there a pittance. I just had to keep my wits about me walking home.

Lottie had finished in the kitchen, bringing through a tray with two mugs of coffee and a plate of sandwiches.

'Oh, thanks, Lottie! I was coming through to make something, but you've beaten me to it.' I said, sounding surprised.

'I was with Alan last night,' said Lottie sounding excited.

'Oh, so you're back together then?' I asked, surprised.

'Well sort of, he found out that his so-called mate hadn't told him the full story about our drinks being spiked at the party,' said Lottie. I thought about the holiday and the four guys from the hotel banging her and the performance on the stage after the competition posing naked not giving a damn, god if he only knew what she had been up to, he would have probably changed his mind again.

'So, are you seeing him again?' I asked, being inquisitive.

'Yeah, I'm seeing him tonight, and I'm going to make it up to him,' said Lottie, smirking with a glint in her eyes. I bet she will; I wondered if he tied her up and shagged her in every orifice there is.

'I am pleased for you, Lottie,' I said, being jealous, she had her shag buddy back.

I was back at the bar for 7 pm shift; the weather was showing signs of freezing with a nip in the air. Walking in, I could see Jerry sitting with Jody and Sarah with a pot of coffee on the table.

'Mothers' meeting?' I said with sarcasm.

'Hi, Liz.' they all shouted in unison. I hung my coat in the backroom before going over to sit with them.

'Coffee is freshly made if you want one,' said Jerry picking up the pot ready to pour me a cup.

'Yeah, go on then. I'll have one.' I said as I sat down next to Jerry. I noticed that all the tables and chairs had been set out with beer mats on the tables ready for the surge of customers coming in.

'Now that you are all here, I need to tell you that you're all doing a brilliant job and with the takings going up tenfold; hence you are being paid a bonus.' Jerry began. 'I must admit I was a be skeptical about your choice of music, but it works, so in future, I will leave you girls to sort out new playlists every week.' continued Jerry smiling at us.

I was wondering where this was leading to, and then he dropped the bombshell. 'Seeing that it is going that well, I was wondering if we could change these uniforms weekly? Giving the customers fresh to look to see my girls in something new,' suggested Jerry sounding us out.

'Hmm, and what do you have in mind?' I asked, sounding curious.

'Well, I thought about a trip to the Anne Summers shop to sort some outfits out,' said Jerry testing us.

'You'll be asking us to wear a maple leaf with tassels on our nipples next?' I said with sarcasm.

'Yeah, the thought did cross my mind,' said Jerry teasing.

'Well, you can fuck off to that,' I said, not mincing my words.

'Only joking,' said Jerry laughing.

'So, who is going to pay for this?' asked Jody.

'Oh, I will be paying for everything,' said Jerry smiling and hoping that we would agree.

'Okay, did you have anything in mind, or can we choose amongst ourselves?' asked Sarah.

'I'll leave that up to you girls, you know what the guys like,' said Jerry grinning as us.

'You do like pushing your luck, Jerry, don't you?' I said, making a point.

'I know you girls like the attention. I've seen you working the customers,' said Jerry, smirking.

'I'll think about it,' I said as he was pushing us too far this time. The girls thought the same and said they would let him know at a later date.

We went to change Jody, and Sarah was not sure about the change of outfits but would go and have a look in the shop to see what there was to suit all of us. I left that with them to report back with the subject closed for now. Despite the night being chilly outside, customers were pouring in. We were playing the music loud, having Jody selecting a few new songs on the list. There was a party of twelve guys come in, one of the guy's stag nights. He was wearing a ball and chain around his neck and was fairly intoxicated as it was getting on for midnight. I noticed one of the guys amongst them was the one I had danced the Lumbada with the night before. I wondered if I could get him to ask me out. Laughing and taking the mick out of each other, they approached the bar. I started to serve them as I pulled the pints. I also chatted, making conversation, the guy I had danced with paid for the round of drinks. As he handed over the money, his fingers rubbed the palm of my hand, sending me a signal he was interested in. I grinned as I met his dark eyes, he grinned back saying he would see me soon. My luck was in tonight.

It was 2 am, and the bar had started to thin out, leaving the twelve guys on the stag night. We started to clean and tidy up, working around customers collecting empty glasses to fill the glasswasher, which took a 20-minute cycle. The guy came up to me being fairly sober, making a change this time of night.

‘Hi, I’m Al,’ he said, standing close to me as I collected the empties.

‘Hi, it’s Liz,’ I said, smiling up at him. His tall frame and muscular built said that he must play rugby; he had that build.

‘Are you going to play the Lumbada for me?’ he asked, grinning.

I smiled, ‘well, if you want, but I’ll have to find it on the playlist.’

‘Go on then. just for me.’ He said, giving me a smirk with a raised eyebrow. I went off to change the setting and pressed play, turning the volume up a tad. He was waiting, my body moulding it into his as we moved with the rhythm. I could feel his hardness underneath his trousers, desperate to enter me, his bedroom eyes enticing me to give in to his manhood. Then we kissed, his soft lips felt arousing, making me wet and my nipples harder. As the music ended, he whispered, asking me to take this further to meet him later. I wasn't sure, but I was missing sex, only having it the once with Jamie since coming back from my holiday of pure pleasure. Could Al give me pleasure? I told it would be 3 am before I finished, but he said he would wait.

3 am was nearly there as Jerry said I should know that Al was waiting for me. I made quick change putting on my coat as I came through to the bar. Stepping outside into the cold air, I buttoned my coat up and stuffed my hands in my pockets. Al put his strong arm around me, hugging me tight as though I would escape. We headed to the car parking at the back of the bar; he was driving. I asked him if he had much to drink.

'No, I've only had a couple of pints.' I was a bit wary about getting into his car.

'It's ok I'll be alright,' he said, reassuring me.

‘Have you far to go?’ I asked, trying to know how far we had to travel.

‘Oh, about 15 minutes away.’ He said, unlocking his car door. ‘Come on, jump in,’ he said, smiling at me. I nervously slid in, waiting for him to set off. He handled the car well as we turned onto the main road heading in the opposite direction to my home. I settled down, knowing I was in safe hands. There was hardly a car in sight as we travelled along the road heading towards the edge of the city.

‘Fuck, how the hell I was going to get back?’ I hoped he would take me home after. He pulled up outside a small block of flats with rows of taller flats either side. Each flat had a parking space at the front, making it easy and not having to tussle for parking. He lived on the top floor with having no lift; we had to climb the stairs; this was a workout on its own.

He unlocked the door, switching the light on as we walked in. The flat was slightly chilly as we entered; his flat was very basic, looking as though it hadn't been lived in. I thought this was a mistake, but I was too far from home. I stood with my coat on as he closed the door behind us. I could feel his hands on my shoulders as he bent down to kiss my neck.

'Aren't you taking your coat off, Liz?' he asked. I slowly started unbuttoning my coat as he took hold of my coat, sliding it off my shoulders and throwing it onto the chair. His hands started to slide down around to my breasts as I could feel the closeness of his body next to mine. He lifted my top as I lifted my arms, he slipped it off, leaving me exposed in my black lacy bra. I shivered slightly, with the temperature being so chilly in the room. He made no comment about the chill. I could now feel his length pressing hard against me, throbbing for attention; he unhooked my bra, my breasts fell into his hands as he squeezed them. His finger and thumb pressed my hard nipples, making me moan with pleasure as my head tilted back onto his chest.

He started to unzip my trousers; they dropped to the floor, leaving me in my lacy undies. His hand ventured to my undies, sliding inside as his fingers entered me. I was aroused and wet, about to come any moment as he kissed my neck. I parted my legs for him to access me more. As he slid off my undies, I was naked in his room; he kept his fingers pressing hard as his other hand on my breast squeezed it so hard that it started to hurt me. I quince a little with the pressure, but he continued ignoring my sound.

He turned me to face him with his fingers still inside as he started to fist pump me hard. My moaning turned in pain as to looked into my eyes, seeing I was hurting. He started to grin. What was he grinning for? Scooping me up, he took me over to the bedroom and threw me on the bed. He was still fully clothed as we entered the chilly bedroom. I was starting to get goosebumps. Even the bedroom was sparse with furniture having a chest of drawers apart from the bed in the room.

This didn't feel right; Al seemed to blow hot and cold, gentle one minute and hurting you the next. I needed to get out of there; I didn't care if I had to walk a mile to get home, I was going. Al was still fully clothed, but as I attempted to get up from the bed, Al pressed his body onto mine, kissing me, but pulling away, he held my hands above my head. Before I knew what he had done, he had one of my wrists tied in a strap that was anchored to the bed. I had not noticed them when he threw me on the bed. When I realized what he was doing, I tried to stop him, but his weight held me down as he tied the other wrist. Fuck, I was in big trouble.

'Al, stop it.' I said, 'I don't do these sorts of things.' I pleaded with him to stop. But Al ignored my pleas while tying my ankles as he spread eagle me over the bed. I was naked and vulnerable; my heart was beating fast, not knowing what he was going to do. The thought of Lottie came back to my thoughts with the four guys from the hotel, but this was different he was a total stranger, and I wasn't sure if he lived there, with the flat being chilly and looking as though the place didn't look lived in. He could see my breathing was heavy, knowing I was stressed, but this didn't make any difference.

Finally, he pulled his trousers down, exposing his hard length, and straddled over me, bringing his length to my face. He moved me into a position to insert his length into my mouth.

'Don't bite, or you will regret it slag. He spat out; his personality had changed. I had pushed my luck too far and was now paying for it. I didn't know whether I would live through this or not. He wound his hand around my hair tightly, pulling hard, forcing his length in my mouth. I could hardly breathe and was gagging with him forcing his length so far inside. He soon came, his hot salty liquid spilt out as some of it spilt out of my mouth, trickling down my chin.

'Swallow, you bitch.' He growled as he pulled out. I swallowed. He moved his length back to my mouth. 'Lick it off, slag, and make sure every drop.' His voice was demanding and vicious.

My brain processed that I was going to die; I was helpless; he couldn't keep me here forever. After I had licked him, he took his hand and wiped the rest on my face and neck, with some going into my hair. He then grabbed me around my throat; my heart pumped hard in total horror was this end. He squeezed slightly as he looked me in the eyes. There was no expression on his face as his dark dead eyes watched me; my eyes looked in horror at him, not knowing what he was going to do next.

‘You dirty fucking slag,’ He whispered, and with that, he started to squeeze my neck tighter until I passed out.

I woke up feeling cold; I realized I was free from my captor, having been fully dressed and lying down in a doorway. I had to get my bearings, where the fuck was I? It was freezing, I realized where I was, it was at the back of the car park of the bar. I gathered myself up and started to walk home, gathering momentum, running looking behind to see if anyone was watching. It was nearly 6 am by the time I got home, fuck that was too close for comfort.

As I closed the door behind me, I sank to the floor and sobbed my heart out; I could have died. He saw me as a slag. It just wasn’t safe anymore. I had learnt my lesson; it stopped here now. I stripped off my clothes padding off to the bathroom I was desperate for a shower, just to wash off his touch and smell. I washed my hair and face several times to wash away his bodily fluids, after which I cleaned my teeth and mouth at least a dozen times, getting his taste out of my mouth. I walked back into my bedroom with my hair wrapped in a towel with one wrapped around my body. I started to dry my hair as I looked in the mirror and noticed bruising around my neck. They were finger marks where he had held my neck and tightened his grip until I passed out.

Fuck, did he think he had killed me? So, he dumped me around the back of the bar. I didn't know what to do, do I go to the police or just leave it and thank my lucky stars I was alive? I asked myself. But the only problem was we hadn't had sex; he had only come in my mouth. I couldn't go through with it; I started to cry as I lay on my bed, curling into a ball, and eventually fell asleep.

It was after midday when I woke, the flat was quiet, and Lottie must have stayed out last night. I tumbled out of bed and threw on jeans and a polo jumper, making my way to the kitchen. I needed a coffee to take his taste from my mouth despite me cleaning my teeth and mouth umpteen times. Alice was due at 4 pm; I just hoped Lottie was going to be back to see her as I didn't feel like entertaining her all by myself.

Lottie was back by 4 pm with Alan in tow. They were all over each other; I felt sick; I needed to be alone with what had happened last night. I wish I could speak to Gus, but I didn't have his number, so I went back into my bedroom to phone Emma, she answered within two rings, I was taken aback with the quick response, being lost for words.

'Oh, hi, Emma. I need to see you, can I come down next weekend to talk to you?' I asked, sounding so desperate.

'Liz, what's wrong? Has something happened? She asked.

'Well sort of, but I don't want to speak on the phone about it,' I said as my voice started to wobble.

'Liz, of course, you can text me when you're at the station, and I'll come and pick you up,' said Emma.

'Oh, Emma, thanks, you're a diamond.' She was about to ask me something else, but the doorbell rang. 'Sorry, Emma, our new flatmate, has just arrived. I'll have to go, so I'll see you Friday night.' I said, ending the call.

I walked through into the living room as Lottie opened the door. Alice was all excited with a big smile on her face, loaded with bags around her. Behind her was a guy gladden with more of Alice's bags. It was raining, which didn't help the move; she had loads of bags, where the hell she was going to put everything? The guy with her was her friend's brother looking as though he was just older enough to drive. It was nearly half an hour before Alice had all her bags in her room; I made the coffee while Lottie entertained everyone as Alice moved in. Once they had finished, I arrived with mugs of coffee, handing them out like sweets. I was glad when the volume of people was down to just the three of us; I had to disappear into my bedroom, I needed to be alone, so I made the excuse I wasn't feeling well.

I laid in bed thinking about my ordeal, if I went to the police people would start to know my business and would think I was a slag. Not only that but my job was about to change, meaning more money, so I wouldn't have to work at the bar. I know Jerry wouldn't be happy about it, but all he cares about was lining his pockets for his wife to spend, 'Fuck him this is my life, and it starts as soon as I get that promotion for the sales manager's vacancy.'

I was up early the following morning having to hide the marks around my neck; luckily, Lottie had given me most of her old make-up, some of which she hadn't used. Applying the concealer and making my face up to blend in,

I found the best top to hide my neck, but I couldn't wear polo as the office soon got too warm. I had to wait a week before I could see Emma. It was difficult holding this inside me as I needed to vent it out but not with Lottie seeing her in that position on holiday.

It was nearly 8 am as I walked into the office, there was no one around, so I headed to the staff kitchen, as I opened the door, I was surprised to see Gus making coffee.

'Oh, I wasn't expecting to see you in here,' I said to him.

'I wasn't expecting to see you either; you're glutton for punishment.' He said as he turned to face me.

'Yeah, you could say that.' I made myself a coffee. 'anyway, why are you in at this time in the morning? I didn't think the top offices started until 9 am.'

'Well, some of us have to keep tabs on the company's finances and have come back earlier than I thought,' he said, smiling and looking at me with his sexy blue eyes.

'Ahan, so loyal to the company,' I said as I sipped my coffee.

'Are you still ok for tomorrow night?' he asked, still smiling with his blue eyes looking at me. I needed to talk to someone about my near-death experience.

'Gus, can I see you tonight? I need to speak to someone.' I said hurriedly as I could hear staff coming in. Gus was surprised but agreed straightway.

'I'll pick you up at 7 pm.'

'Yes, that's great, thanks.' I walked out back into the sales office. The day went quickly with the phones ringing nonstop. Matt had given us a new list of stocks to clear, so the calls kept on coming through the day. I went into sales mode, pushing to sell the clearance stocks.

I managed to leave on time; I was the first out the door rushing home. Lottie wasn't home yet, but Alice was as I could hear her in her bedroom singing along to her playlist. She had her work cut out, finding room to put away all the stuff she had brought with her. I made coffee and a sandwich taking them into my bedroom. I switched on my TV while I ate my sandwich, after which I nipped into the bathroom to have a shower. To feel more comfortable, I slipped on jeans and a polo neck jump, as I waited for Gus to pick me up.

He was on time; I ran down the steps as he waited for me to climb into his car.

'So, where would you like to go?' he asked.

'Oh anywhere,' I said, not bothered.

'How would you feel coming back to my place?' asked Gus, knowing I wanted to talk.

'Yeah, whatever.' I said, 'I need to talk.'

He started the engine and pulled out knowing I had something on my mind, he looked concerned for me but didn't speak until we had arrived at his apartment, I was taken in the views of the quays. It was the posh end of the city, god his mate must have some money working abroad.

We took the lift to the top floor, my heart pounding with the thought of my near-death experience. Gus noticed I was panicking and said that we could go somewhere else.

'No, it's ok,' I said, trying to put the thought to the back of my mind. He opened the door; the room was huge, with views overlooking the quays and the city. It was like being in a five-star hotel.

'God, this must have cost your mate a bit,' I said, looking around touching things as I walked on.

'Mm a bit,' said Gus, not making anything about it. 'Would you like a drink?' asked Gus, 'coffee or something stronger?'

‘Oh, coffee is fine,’ I said as I walked over to the view in front of me. What a view I thought, Gus had a good mate, trusting him to stay while he was away. He brought through the mugs of coffee and placed them on the coffee table and sat on the sofa, waiting for me to start talking. I walked over and sat next to him, taking my coffee sipping it slowly.

‘Oh, Gus, I don’t know where to begin.’ I burst into tears. He hugged me as I snuggled up to him, kicking off my shoes and putting my feet, folding them back on the sofa. The heat coming from his body warmed me as I could hear his heartbeat. Why was he interested in seeing me? I was just a slag at the end of the day. I needed love in my life and found it briefly with Luke, but didn’t know where to find it now I was home? So, I went back to my old ways, and I nearly got myself killed.

Gus waited until I finished sobbing. I started to tell him my whole sex life, including the experiences I had on holiday with the pleasuring and falling in love with the guy I had met. With another couple of coffees, I had told him everything. Gus was silent; I was thinking, I had made a mistake telling him. Was that the guy you were dancing with when I saw you? Asked Gus as I could see his facial expressions tighten.

‘I shouldn’t have done it,’ I said, knowing I shouldn’t have done it. ‘I just want to be loved.’ I sniffed as a tear escaped from my eye. Gus hugged me, kissing the top of my head.

‘You are loved,’ he said.

‘Yeah, and who does?’ I asked, not knowing what he meant by it.

‘I love you, Liz, from the day I saw you in the staff kitchen all in a fluster,’ said Gus hugging me and kissing me on the head again.

'Gus, how can you say it now when I have just told you what I have done?' I looked into his blue eyes.

'Liz, it doesn't matter what you have done; I want to look after you, to be there when I get home, to be there next to me when I wake up in the mornings. To love you for who you are.'

'Gus, you work at the same place, and what happens if it doesn't work out? I have been down this road before.'

'Liz, you have been meeting the wrong guys.' He said.

'I do like you very much, but I'm not sure, Gus. I don't know much about you, do I?'

'So, what would you like to know?' he asked.

'Well for a start I don't know your last name, how old are you? Where your parents live? Do you have any hobbies? Are you or have you been married? oh, lots of things.' I babbled on.

'Well, for starters, I am 35 years old, and single nearly got married. My father died when I was 25 years old, and my mother remarried. I went to university and shagged a lot of women, but now I have found the right girl.' said Gus hugging me tightly.

'Oh, so you've found someone,' I asked, sounding disappointed.

'Liz, you sound disappointed.' he frowned.

'Mm, I thought we could see each other occasionally.'

'Liz, you're my girl. I don't want anyone else.' Gus hugged me, lifting my chin up and gently kissed me on the lips. There was a connection; I started to get aroused despite my ordeal from that night.

'Gus, can we take it slowly?' I said, looking into his piercing blue eyes.

'Liz just takes as much time as you need. I can wait for you,' said Gus kissing me more passionately. He had stirred something inside me, his kiss had meaning, and I needed to explore him. I sat up needing to go to the bathroom; Gus pointed me in the right direction as I padded across, barefoot. On opening the bathroom door, I met with an amazing sight; it was like being back in Luke's hotel room with a 5-star rating. There was a large walk-in power shower and a bath to fit half a dozen people in. The whole bathroom was tiled from top to bottom in speckle light brown tiles with a dark brown border.

I padded back, having splashed my face with cold water and was feeling a lot better. Gus had made some more coffee, which was waiting for me when I came back from the bathroom.

'Are you ok, Liz?' he asked.

'Yes, thanks.' I went over to straddle him kissing him on the lips with passion. His arms wrapped around me as he lifted me and laid me onto the long white leather sofa. He started to kiss my neck then stopped as he saw the marks around my neck.

'Liz, my sweet, why don't you go to the police and report him?'

'No, I can't. I don't want people to know what's happened, especially at work, they will judge me, and I would be embarrassed.' I said, not wanting to discuss this any further.

'Liz, he can't get away with it,' said Gus gritting his teeth as the muscles in his jawline flinched.

'Please, Gus, leave it. I need to put it behind me,' I said to end the conversation of the matter. I kissed him again as I moved my hands into his unruly blond hair holding tight and pushing his head harder as his lips met mine.

'Liz, I've been waiting for this moment since the day I saw you,' whispered Gus as we started to exchange tongues. My wetness was full-on I needed his naked body next to mine.

'Gus, make love to me,' I whispered. Gus scooped me up, carrying me with no effort to the bedroom as he pushed the door open with his foot to expose a modern four-poster bed which blended in with the rest of the furniture in the room; it was like another room in a 5-star hotel.

We stood next to the bed as we slowly peeled each other's clothing, kissing our exposed parts until we were both naked. Looking at his taut, muscular body with his length bursting for its release, I needed to give him his pleasure. I had already come with his touch and kisses; he stopped me from going down on him. He was pleasuring me just the way Luke had done; he was experienced in that department.

Scooping me up to lay me on the bed, he laid over me as he started kissing his way down, cupping my breasts and rubbing his finger and thumb over my hard nipples. It was overwhelming as I moaned in pleasure, calling his name. I was coming over and over again, arching my back in ecstasy; he parted my legs to explore my wetness with his mouth. I kept on coming I was so responsive to his tongue and lips. I felt so relaxed and safe with him, as it showed with my wetness. My hands clasped his hair as he pleasured me; I pulled him up, clasping his hair to make him kiss me to share the taste of my come in my mouth and for him to enter me and release his pleasure. Within seconds he had come.

'Oh, Gus, you are my perfect man. I love you so much.' It slipped out of my mouth, and then I realized what I had said.

'Liz, you are my perfect girl, and I will protect you and love you.' we kissed each other passionately and held each other in our arms in silence for a few minutes.

'Gus, can we keep this between us for a while?' I asked.

'Hmm, if that's what you want, my sweet,' said Gus squeezing me as he kissed me gently on the lips.

'Good,' I started to go down on him, kissing his lips first, working my way down to his length in need of attention. I placed my hands on the inside of his thighs, moving them slowly back and forth; he opened his leg wider, giving me full access to his balls. I licked them as I caressed them with my hands, kissing and sucking gently as he started to moan in pleasure. His length grew as I slid my tongue onto his length, flicking his tip, making it sweep slightly as I licked it off.

Gus called my name as I pleased him; his fingers were inside me as my wetness came. His full length came alive as I sucked him hard, giving him his pleasure. I swallowed his hot salty liquid, as he came, not spilling a drop, I needed to taste him. He brought me up, turning me over as he kissed me passionately, cupping my breasts and rubbing his finger and thumb between my hard nipples.

Working my nipples, he worked on my breasts, massaging them.

'Gus, pull my nipples hard,' I demanded. He obliged; I came with the response as he pulled. 'keep pulling my nipples.' I demanded, he responded, and the sensation hit me again, bringing me into multiple orgasms calling his name. He slid down, drinking in my wetness; he was killing me with pleasure. After licking me dry, he came up, giving me a taste of my poison.

It was getting on for midnight as we lay snuggled up to each other, his leg and arm over my naked body. We chatted about work, and then he asked me about the job at the bar.

'I have to do this; it pays for the extras as my salary doesn't cover extras, that's why I share flat,' I said.

'Why don't you apply for Matt's job as Sales Manager? It's a hell of lot more money, plus benefits with meeting clients and conferences,' said Gus sounding me out.

'How do you know about that?' I asked as Matt had only spoken with me a few days ago about leaving.

'Oh, I get to know about everything that goes on in the company. I am finance, remember?' said Gus kissing me on the shoulder.

'I suppose you're right.' I said, 'but I'm not sure.' I said, sighing.

'Come on, Liz, you can sell sand to the Arabs, you're the top girl in sales. Not only that, but the list Matt gives out every Monday morning, you sell 99 per cent of it,' said Gus giving me confidence.

'Yeah, the money would be handy, plus I could give up the bar, and depend on the salary, I can have a place of my own,' I said now, convinced that it would be the right choice to make.

Gus took me home, not that I wanted to leave him, but we both had work in the morning and didn't want to be seen together. I also needed to change my clothes like jeans and a polo neck jump wouldn't go down very well in the office. I was so happy I had found my perfect guy. As I jumped out of the car, I heard Gus.

‘Liz, you still on for tomorrow night as planned?’ asked Gus grinning.

‘I wouldn’t miss it for the world.’ I reached over and kissed him passionately on the lips. He watched me open the door to the flat before driving off, ‘God, he’s so thoughtful.’ I thought. I laid in my bed, unable to sleep thinking of him. I eventually drifted off the sleep with a smile on my face.

I was at work by 8 am despite having a late night. I switched on my computer, shoving my bag in my desk, I took my coat hanging it in up, in the recess in the office. I needed a coffee; there wasn’t anyone in as I pushed the staff kitchen door open. Filling the kettle, I had to wait until the kettle boiled, being the first to use it. I prepared my mug, waiting for the kettle to boil, as I waited, the kitchen door opened, and two strong arms enveloped me around the waist, kissing my neck. I knew it was Gus by his kiss and his touch; I turned around.

'I've missed you,' I said, kissing him softly on the lips.

'Hmm me too,' said Gus kissing me on the neck, I moaned he was arousing me.

'Oh, Gus, you'll make me come.' I moaned.

'I wanted you to,' said Gus as he cupped my breasts.

'Gus, the staff will be in soon,' I said, desperately wanting to carry this on but had to stop. Within a few minutes, we heard the outside door open. I quickly straightened my blouse and poured the boiling water into my mug, giving Gus a quick kiss on the lips as I walked out in the sales office to start work.

My thoughts were with Gus having that intimate moment in the staff kitchen and knowing he was not far away. As soon as 8.30 am, arrived the phones had switched over and started to ring. The sales office had a large electronic board displaying the number of calls taken, answered, and waiting to indicate the workload; the sales team could see at a glance how busy they were. The calls started to die down around 3 pm as Anne went off to make a coffee. We all started to banter each other as Anne came back excited to tell everyone that a notice had gone on the board advertising for a Sales Manager.

'Did anyone know there's a sales manager's job on the notice board? Says Anne getting everyone's attention.

Everyone looked up, including me, even though I knew.

'I didn't know that Matt was leaving,' said Anne as she turned to me.

'Yeah, that's a big surprise. I thought he would be here forever,' I said, making it sound I didn't know.

'Yeah, so did I.,' said Anne turning back to her desk. Matt could hear chatter in the office as he came in.

‘So, is it true you are leaving us?’ said Anne waiting to hear his reply.

‘Yes, I’m going to another branch to be head of sales,’ he said, smiling now that his job had been advertised.

‘So, if anyone is interested in applying, please feel free to do so, and I’ll sign your application for HR to process your application.’ He announced before he disappeared back into his office, there was chatter about who was going to apply for the job.

‘Are you going to apply for the job, Liz? You’re supposed to be number one seller,’ said Carl with some sarcasm.

‘Fuck off, Carl,’ I shouted back as the banter started. Did I need this? I had to give this some thought.

I was out of the door by 5 pm, leaving some of the staff on the phones dealing with customer enquiries. Matt walked out of the building with me as we were now in an area where there was no one around.

‘Liz, you have to apply for the job; the company needs you,’ he said, selling me the job.

‘I don’t know yet. I need to think about it.’ I said as we faced each other.

‘Look, just apply to see what the deal is, then make up your mind,’ said Matt as he turned to walk away as we could hear someone walking near. I continued to walk home, why was the company so interested in me apply for the job? Still, the same as Matt said I could apply and see what they were offering.

When I got home, Alice was in the living room with an unknown guy; he was thick-set, having a shaven head with tattoos over his arms.

‘Hi, Alice, who is your friend?’ I asked, coming into the living room.

‘This is Marcus, my boyfriend,’ said Alice giggling as she hung on to his arm.

‘Hi,’ said Marcus. His dark eyes were looking me up and down as though he was undressing me. I wasn’t sure about this guy, but time will tell, I thought.

‘So, when do you start working then, Alice?’ I asked curiously that she hadn’t been working since she came on Sunday evening.

‘Not until Monday it just gives me a bit of time to adjust,’ said Alice. Marcus sat quietly as Alice spoke.

‘What do you do then, Marcus?’ I asked.

‘I’m a bouncer in the city centre for a night club,’ said Marcus.

‘Whoa, you must have your hands full, then?’ I said, smiling at him.

‘Yeah, just a bit,’ he said, ending the conversation.

There was something about him; I wasn't sure what, but there was something.

Chapter Thirteen:

I asked Alice and her boyfriend if they would like a coffee; they both said no. I walked into my bedroom after taking off my coat and throwing it on the side with my bag. I brought my coffee back into my bedroom, taking off my work clothes to get ready for tonight with Gus. I nipped into the bathroom for a quick shower before I decided what I was going to wear. I needed something not too casual; he was taking me out to dinner.

I thought about my short black dress with black lacy underwear and to complete the look with suspender and fishnets. Or would that be too trashy? Doubt crept in. No, I better go in black trousers with a coloured blouse. I was not sure. It showed some cleavage, and I was okay with that. I applied my make-up while the TV was on, but I did not take any notice of it. I was buzzing with excitement, for now, I finally had a guy who loved me, despite working at the same place as me, but luckily he worked in a different department making it easier not to cross each other's paths.

Gus was on time as I was waiting for him. Alice was in her room with Marcus as I could hear them talking. Lottie wasn't home yet, but as I opened the door, Lottie was just coming in.

'Hi yeah, babes,' said Lottie buzzing.

'Hi, Lottie I'm just going out.' I waved, but she didn't respond as I left. Something must have happened, I thought, making my way to Gus's car. I opened the car door and slid in, kissing Gus desperately on his lips.

'Oh, Gus, I've been dying to see you all day,' I told him.

'Mm so have I,' said Gus in a sexy voice, kissing my lips as he cupped my face in his hands.

Gus selected first gear and pulled out into the road heading out of the city.

'Where are you taking me?' I asked.

'Just a village pub, they do lovely meals.' smiled Gus as he changed the gear.

'I'm hungry! I haven't had anything to eat today.' I said.

'You should always have a big breakfast in the morning to start the day,' said Gus making a point.

'Yeah, I know, but I don't feel that hungry in the morning.' I rolled my eyes. Within half an hour we were outside the pub, it was quaint outside and inside, only having a small dining area where we sat in the far corner.

We sat down while Gus ordered a bottle of wine; the menu had a good selection to choose from. The waitress came back with the wine. Gus asked her to leave it as he would pour the wine. We ordered our meal, and while we waited, Gus poured me a full glass with a small glass for himself. We chatted over the meal, as I brought up the conversation of the sales team knowing about Matt leaving with his job on the notice board.

'You are going to apply, aren't you, Liz?' asked Gus sounding serious.

'Hmm, I think so. I'll see what they have to offer.' I said with a forced smile.

'Good.' Gus smiled back as he sipped his wine.

'Oh, I forgot to mention, I'm going down to London on Friday evening to see Emma for the weekend,' I said, and my face lit up.

'What did Jerry say about that?' asked Gus surprised I was giving two evenings work up.

'I don't know yet. I haven't told him, but I know he won't be very happy about it.' I said, shrugging my shoulders.

'Oh,' he said, raising his eyebrows.

We left the pub heading straight back to Gus's apartment next to the quays. We couldn't keep our hands off each other, by the time we were through his apartment door we were both half undressed, he had made me come multiples of times as we drove back from the pub, his hands and fingers working their magic on my sensitive body. I made things even as he drove down the motorway, I unzipped him taking out his length and sucking hard making him swerve as he came moaning in pleasure. Smirking, I swallowed my dessert of his salty hot liquid, licking him dry before zipping him back up.

By the time we hit the bed, we were naked with our clothes, leading a trial from the apartment door. Gus was down on me his tongue and fingers working their magic as I kept coming. I was so sensitive, my body ached, my breathing heavy with pleasure. I stopped him as we rolled over, I straddled him and kissed him hard on the lips.

'Oh Gus, I can't get enough of you,' I whispered, breathing heavy. I slid down as his length was waiting for me; I devoured his length, making him come straight away as he called my name in pleasure. I swallowed his hot liquid and licked him dry once more. He rolled me over straddling,

'Liz, you don't know what you're doing to me.' breathed Gus as he kissed me softly on the lips tasting his salty liquid. Our tongues were tying themselves together, sucking in each other. We both moaned in pleasure in unison. He started kissing my neck down to my breasts as my hard nipples waited for his attention. He massaged my breasts, and I moaned,

'Gus pull my nipples hard.' My voice was merely a whisper. His fingers and thumbs took hold of my nipples, pulling them both harder and harder; I responded by the sensation I was feeling by releasing my orgasm, hard.

We were pleasuring each other so much; sweat was pouring off the both of us as we headed into the bathroom, turning the walk-in shower on. The water-cooled our bodies and washed away our bodily fluids; we washed and pleasured each other as the water ran over our bodies. It was nearly 3 am.

'God! Look at the time,' I said surprised; the time had passed in a blur.

'Stay, I'll drop you off at 7 am,' asked Gus looking at me with his piercing blue eyes.

'How can I refuse? I can't get enough of you, Gus.' I kissed him softly on his lips.

'Me neither,' said Gus as we both curled up together on the bed and tried to get some sleep.

Gus took me home by 7 am, we only had a couple of hours sleep together, making loving had taken its toll, my body ached all over, but the ache was a good ache, so I didn't mind it. Gus asked if I would see him the following evening. I was over the moon needing more of him; I was like a hormonal teenager. I kissed him on the lips tracing my tongue on his lips and said 'Until tonight, lover' as I quickly jumped out of the car before I came in my undies.

I ran up the steps to the flat unlocking the door. Gus waited until I went in before driving off. The flat was silent as I entered the living room; I needed a coffee to make me human after only having less than a couple of hours sleep. I took my mug of coffee into my bedroom, my make-up needed freshening up, I cleansed my face of make-up ready to re-apply fresh, but first I needed to have a quick shower. I finished my coffee before jumping into the shower; I washed my hair as I thought about Gus,

God, I should have started seeing him the first day I met him, but I was embarrassed with the love bites Jo had given me that night.

It was dead at 8.30 am when I arrived at work, a few colleagues commented on my time.

'Hmm, late-night shagging Liz?'

'Oh, piss off,' I said, knowing the real truth. I needed a coffee so quickly dumping my coat and bag on my desk; I rushed to get one. I had to wait in the staff kitchen, looked like everyone decided they needed a coffee. Once I had made my coffee, I headed back to my desk to hang up my coat in the recess. The phones were starting to ring as the electronic board lit up, indicating the number of calls coming in. I longed for 5 pm to come around, knowing I would see Gus at 7 pm.

Anne piped up in the office, 'so whose applying for Matt's job then?' she asked her voice being heard above the noise in the office.

There were a handful of answers, ‘And what about you, Liz? You would be good at it.’ said Anne grinning at me.

‘I don’t know. I might just put an application in and see what happens.’ I said, not making much of it.

‘Well, the applications have to be in by the end of next week,’ said Anne.

‘Oh, so I’ve got some time then,’ I said, making nothing of it. But unbeknown to them I was going to be offered the job.

We had half an hour for a lunch break, I took mine first as I needed some fresh air and to get away from the office talks about Matt’s job, not only that I needed something to eat with not having anything to eat since last night apart from Gus’s cock. I could do with him now and suck him hard, I thought. Only 5 minutes down the road, I nipped into the café for a coffee and a salad sandwich. I was walking back to work when I saw Gus; he was talking on his phone. He saw me approaching him as he cut his call short.

'Hello my love,' I said grinning and licking my lips at him.

'Hi sweetheart, I don't usually see you out this time of day,' asked Gus, holding me as he kissed me softly on the lips.

'I know, I needed something to eat, but I was thinking now I've seen you something else came to my mind.' I grinned and licked his lips.

'Liz, you're turning me on sweetheart, it's not good for work,' said Gus turning as he could see a couple of managers coming his way but luckily they hadn't seen him. I was about to say something when he walked off, leaving me standing there.

Had I said something wrong? But then I saw the two managers walking towards me, they were chatting and walked straight passed me oblivious to their surroundings even to acknowledge me. Whoa, that was close, no wondered he legged it. I was thinking about Matt's job, would these managers speak to me or stub me as most managers seem to have their click of people they associated with.

By the time I had got back to my desk I had eaten my lunch, the phones were constantly ringing once you had put the phone down, you were picking it up again back into sales mode. The afternoon went quickly, and eventually, the phones died down, allowing me a quick escape out at 5 pm. My thoughts returned to Gus, he was picking me up tonight to go back to his place, so I thought I would wear a short black dress with no undies.

There wasn't anyone in the flat; having the place to myself, I walked around naked between the bathroom and my bedroom. The thought struck me that it would be nice to have a place of my own. I was still on my own when Gus arrived to pick me up at 7 pm.

I ran down the steps to the car; I could see Gus was smiling.

'Hello, sweetheart,' said Gus. I jumped in giving him a passionate kiss on the lips,

'How's my lover tonight?' I asked, looking into his piercing blue eyes.

'I'm better for seeing you gorgeous.' We were soon back in his apartment half undressed, panting as he entered me in the elevator pushing against the side as I curled my legs around him with our tongues entwining, Gus pushed me against the side of the elevator getting his full length pushing hard inside me. It released my wetness straight away; I called out his name as I panted heavily, it was a good thing I wasn't wearing anything underneath my dress.

Our clothes trialed through the apartment to the bedroom; he scooped me up going down on me, making me come instantly,

'Oh, Gus, you're so good. I love you so much; you make me so happy. I was constantly moaning. My nipples were hard as stones as soon as I got into his car. He knew they needed pulling as his finger and thumbs took hold of them, pulling as I moaned louder coming over and over again while he drank my wetness.

'Gus you're going to kill me doing that.' I said panting and moaning, 'but what a way to go.' I said, loving every minute of it. He came back up to share my wetness as we kissed exchanging my wetness in my mouth. Rolling him over I straddles him as I looked into his sexy blue eyes, he knew what was coming as I started to kiss him slowly heading down to his balls, licking them as I squeezed them slightly making his length rise. I continued kissing and licking as a little tear slipped from his tip, I licked it dry.

He was moaning my name, and I knew he was about to come, taking his length in my mouth I sucked him hard, within seconds he had come. I held it in my mouth coming up to share with him; he devoured my mouth as we drank it in together, his finger and thumb were still pulling my nipples, making me come on him.

We gasped for air, 'Liz, do you have to go down to London on Friday?' he whispered, looking me in the eye.

'Yeah, I can't back out now, Emma's expecting me, not only that when I rang her, I thought I nearly died I needed someone to talk to, so I ran to her, I didn't know your phone number. She knows I was upset but wouldn't tell her over the phone.' I explained.

'Oh Liz, I should have given you my phone number from the start,' said Gus now giving it a thought.

'Why don't you come with me?' I offered, smiling at him.

'I wish I could, but I have to stay behind on Friday as it's month-end and we need the figures ready for the board meeting on Monday,' said Gus as he reached over rubbing my lips with his.

We were hot, sweating with having so much pleasure with both our wetness shared through each other's mouths. Gus scooped me up in a fireman's lift over his shoulder and padded over to the bathroom. He switched the shower on as we entered, the cool water pouring over us. Gus seemed to have that same high sex drive as Luke; I wondered if he had other pleasures in mind.

Gus was out of the shower first saying he was going to make some coffee. I continued to dry my hair having been drenched under the large shower head, rounding the large bath towel around me I padded out into the kitchen where Gus had just made the coffee, slipping my arms around his waist I hugged him pressing my breasts against his back.

'Why can't I get enough of you, Gus?' I said, kissing his back as my hand slid down to his length. He was ready like a button being pressed on. As he spun around, my towel dropped to the floor; he turned me around bending me over the kitchen counter, entering me from the back as he pulled on my nipples, making us both come together.

'Liz, we are going to kill each at this rate,' said Gus panting as he kissed my shoulder.

'But it's good.' though I said sounding sexy.

We drank our coffee while looking out over the view from the apartment, there were no blinds or curtains, being at the top which towered above the other buildings that surrounded it. The glass was made discreetly, you could see out, but no one could see in. That gave you a full view over the quays and the city with no obstacles to move.

'Gus, why don't you come down to London on Saturday, if you have to stay behind on Friday?' I asked.

'Yes, if you want me to, it will give you some time to chat with Emma,' said Gus smiling at me.

'Brilliant,' I said, kissing him on the lips nearly spilling my coffee on Gus.

It was 2 am, but I didn't want to go home, I wanted to stay with Gus. We both went back to the bedroom but this time, settling into bed entwined in each other, soaking heat of our bodies as we both fell asleep. I panicked as I woke up facing the bedside clock. It said at 7.45 am. Gus had his arm and leg over my body, weighing me down, as I struggled to move, Gus woke up, wondering what my panic was about. I babbled on about the time and needing to get to work.

Gus didn't make much of the time glancing at the clock.

'Gus look at the time.' I squeaked 'I'm going to be late for work.' I said, collecting my dress off the floor, lucky I wasn't wearing any underwear, slipping on my shoes and coat I was ready to go. Gus was amused watching me in a panic, with a casual approach, he slipped on his joggers and trainers; we headed down to his car.

'Fuck, I'm going to be late for work, I've never been late, it will go on my file for being late, it's alright for you lot in the top office coming in later,' I said, twiddling my fingers and thumbs wanting to get back to change and rush off to work. The traffic was a little heavy, making the journey taking longer to get back; it was nearly 8.25 am when Gus dropped me off.

With a quick kiss I said I would text him now I had his number, jumping out of the car, I ran into the flat as Lottie was coming out.

‘Morning, Liz,’ said Lottie as we passed on the steps. I ignored her as I was blinkered knowing I had to get to work as quickly as possible.

I slipped on the nearest thing suitable for the office, making my way out of the flat trotting along the pavement, having to wait to cross the roads as I made my way to work. This was the wrong time of day, the traffic was slowly running, and I had to dodge the cars to get to the other side of the road, with cars breaking hard and drivers shouting abuse, but I didn’t care I needed to get to work.

It was nearly 9.15 am when I walked through the door; I could hear the phones ringing. I opened the sales office door, some of my colleagues glanced up while they were on the phone speaking to the customers, while others made rude jesters about my love life. I ignored them hanging my coat in the recess, dumping my bag on the desk and headed to the staff kitchen for a much-needed coffee. It was ok for Gus living nearer to work starting later in the morning. I slumped in my chair as I sat my coffee on the desk and placed my bag under my desk. I logged in into my computer, and once it was on, I started taking calls.

Anne gave me a look as to ask why I was late? But I shrugged it off ignoring her as we both answered calls.

It was nearly 1.30 pm, and I needed something to eat, with a lull in the phone call I disappeared picking my bag up and headed out to pick a sandwich from the nearby café down the road.

'Are you going to the café, Liz?' piped up Anne as I was grabbing my coat and bag.

'Yeah, why?' I asked.

'I'll come with you,' she said as she got up from her seat and picked up her purse from her desk draw.

'Oh fuck,' I thought she would be asking me questions the nosey cow. 'Yeah ok, I'm going now.' I said wanting to avoid her questions, but as we got out of the door she started; 'Fuck Liz, just say yes and no in the right places.'

'So, what made you late this morning, Liz?' she asked with a grin on her face expecting me to tell her.

'My alarm didn't go off,' I said, hoping she was that gullible to believe me sounding as normal as possible.

I heard a text come through on my phone, I quickly glanced at it, it was Gus, and he had already sent me six texts since I had been at work.

'Anne, will you get me a sandwich? I'll catch you up in a moment.' I said, handing a note from my bag.

'Oh yeah, talking to lover boy, are we?' said Anne grinning as she took the note. I ignored her comment as she walked off, as soon as she was out of ears shot I phoned Gus on his mobile. He answered in two rings,

'Hello sweetheart, are you having a good day?' he said, I could guess he was smiling down the phone.

‘No, I’m having a bad day, doesn’t help to be late and to have to put up with comments about my sex life,’ I said sighing.

‘I miss you, sweetheart; will I see you tonight,’ said Gus.

‘You know I work on Thursdays, not only that I have to tell Jerry I won’t be on Friday and Saturday night; he will go ballistic when I tell him.’ I sighed.

‘Well, when you get the manager’s job, you won’t have to anymore, and you can spend more time with me,’ said Gus sounding sensible in one way but selfish for him. But he was right about giving the part-time job at the bar with having enough money on a Sales Managers salary, and now I had found my perfect guy.

‘Would you like me to pick you up after work at 11.30 pm?’ asked Gus sounding sincere.

'That would be lovely thanks,' I said, knowing where it would lead to later after.

'I've got to go, sweetheart, I'll call you later.' He said as he ended the call.

As I walked towards the café, Anne was coming out holding two packs of sandwiches, 'here' she said, 'Which one would you like?'

'Oh, it doesn't matter,' I said as she handed me my change from the sandwich. As we walked back to the office, she started talking about Matt's job; she was going to apply as she informed me that so were a few others in the office.

'So, are you applying then?' asked Anne trying to probe me for information.

'Probably just to see what the package they are offering,' I said, making nothing of it, knowing I had it in the bag. She started babbling on about colleagues who she knew had applied already. I wasn't listening and just agreed with her. By the time we had got back to the office, I had eaten my sandwich and needed a coffee to swill it down with, so I headed straight to the staff kitchen. Luckily the kettle had boiled taking me a few minutes before I was back at my desk.

I left just after 5 pm despite being late this morning; I had no option having to be at the bar for 7 pm and let Jerry know I wouldn't be in on Friday and Saturday night. I was dreading him exploding telling me I can't do this to him. But needs must, and I had more or less pleaded with Emma to come down to London to talk to her. No one was in when I got home, not even Alice. I had only spoken to her a few times since she had been here with the last conversation, we had she was with the bodyguard boyfriend of hers, Mr. Talkative.

After three mugs of coffee, I headed out to the bar. Jerry was sure going to go ballistic when I told him. But if I were sick, he would still have to cope without me.

Jerry was in the backroom as I hung my coat on the hanger, now was the time to tell him. As I had thought he went ballistic saying that it was only not so long ago I had been off for two weeks and was taking the piss. I kept apologizing to him, Jody and Sarah could hear the raised voices coming from the backroom, thank god they came in as Jerry walked out muttering under his breath.

'What's all that about?' asked Jody surprised that Jerry had been shouting at me.

'I've just told him I wouldn't be in tomorrow and Saturday night.'

'Oh, dear,' said Sarah.

'Yeah, it's done now,' I said as I walked out into the bar. I could hear Jerry banging about in the kitchen shouting at the staff, why was he taking it so badly?

I was glad we didn't have to wear our sexy uniforms. Now that I have seen myself and had acted like a slag, I felt ashamed, Jerry was going to whistle and will have to find someone else soon. I kept watching the door, seeing if that guy Al would turn up again, I was glad Gus was picking me up after work knowing I would be safe in his arms. It was nearly 10.30 pm as I was filling the glasswasher when someone called my name. I turned, standing at the bar was Jo from the rigs.

'Hey, you're back then?' I said, making conversation.

'Yeah, I got three weeks to leave.' He smiled at me.

'It is a pint, Jo?' I asked, walking over to pick up an empty glass.

‘Yeah, and one for yourself?’ said Jo as he pulled wade of notes from his back pocket.

‘Thanks, I’ll have orange juice, so what are you doing for the three weeks off?’ I asked, keeping the conversation going.

‘You could keep me company,’ he said grinning at me.

I smiled back at him and said that I don’t think my boyfriend would like that.

‘Oh, I’m sure we could share you,’ he said, sounding like I was a piece of meat being passed around for shag.

I walked away to serve other customers; I just hoped Gus would be there soon not having to wait for him to pick me up; I didn’t want Jo hanging around me when he turned up. The empty glasses needed collecting; I couldn’t see Jody or Sarah in the bar area, where the fuck were they? Seeing that there was no one waiting to be served; I went out into the bar area to collect the empty glasses. I could see Jo from the corner of my eye watching me walking around the room collecting the empties, placing them on the bar counter. Jo was stood at the bar where the glasswasher was stood, and with having to fill the machine, I had no option in avoiding him.

Jo was watching while I filled the glasswasher.

'Why don't you come back with me tonight so I can give you a good fucking and you can have the pleasure to suck me off?' said Jo sounding cocky and slightly drunk. As I turned around to say something Gus was stood next to him, my mouth dropped fuck did he hear that?

'You will have to wait your turn mate; she's got me tonight,' said Gus raising his left eyebrow. I didn't know what to say and finished filling the glasswasher. It was 11.30 pm. I was ready to go, seeing that I hadn't seen much of Jody and Sarah for the last hour. I quickly picked my coat and bag from the back room and came back into the bar area where Gus was waiting. I kissed him gently on the lips as he enveloped me, hugging me tightly before releasing me as we left the bar for home.

I was relieved the evening shift had finished now Gus was by my side in the car.

'Liz, will you stop working at the bar for me?' asked Gus sounding serious.

'Why? what's brought this on?' I asked, turning to look at him while he was driving.

'Because I love you and I don't like guys like him saying things to you, you don't need it,' said Gus getting slightly agitated.

'I know Gus, but I can't at the moment. I need the extra cash.' I said, trying to justify my excuse.

‘Why don’t you move in with me?’ asked Gus as he placed his hand on my thigh.

‘No, Gus it’s not that easy, is it? we both work at the same place and what if something happened between us?’ I said in a whisper hoping it never came to that.

‘Don’t think that Liz, I won’t let it happen,’ said Gus running his hand up and down my thigh.

‘I am starting to have feelings for you, and I don’t want to lose you, but I’m concerned about work.’ I voiced my concern.

‘Never worry about work, that will sort itself out,’ said Gus as he turned his vehicle parking it in private parking space provided for the apartment block.

I didn’t take it any further as we entered the lift, Gus grabbed hold of me kissing my neck as he unbuttoned my blouse and bra to gain a hold on my hard nipples, tugging gently making me moan in pleasure and gradually harder as I felt the sensation kick in making me find my release. Gus knew me now, knowing the right buttons to press to make me come quickly. He just about had me undressed by the time we entered his apartment. As we entered the bedroom, I stripped him off demanding to stand; still, he obeyed, and I told him to lie on the back. He was smirking knowing what I was going to do; we seemed to start knowing what each other needed, and had started enjoying every second of pleasure and lovemaking. Gus was already hard, so taking him by surprise I took is length straight into my mouth, sucking hard, making him come straight away as he moaned. I held on to his hot salty liquid bringing it to his lips as we shared our love.

His finger and thumb on my nipples pulled them as the sensation kicked in making me come. He rolled me over, going down to eat and drink, and working his magic fingers as I came. We both panted and sweated as though we had been working out in the gym, but I loved it, and yes, I was slowly falling in love with him.

It was getting on for nearly 2 am; Gus shoved me into the shower turning it on full pressure as the spray hit our bodies, washing away the smell of our hot bodies and bodily fluids. We had another session of pleasuring each other before Gus escaped to make coffee. I could have stayed all night, but I didn't want to be late again, as this would lead me to a warning from the HR department for timekeeping. Gus was lucky working flexible hours but usually came in for 9 am with that odd occasion I met him in the staff kitchen at 8 am that morning I was in early. By the time Gus drove me home, it was nearly 3.30 am, at least I was going to get some sleep making sure the alarm was set for 7 am.

I was wide awake at 6 am as I rolled overlooking at the clock, I couldn't get comfortable now I was wide awake, so I decided to get up and go to work early and catch up on my emails. I walked to work and called into the café, getting a takeaway coffee and a breakfast bar to eat. I was at work for 7 am; the place was silent as I walked in having the place to myself giving me time to think about what Gus had said about me moving in with him and to stop working at the bar. I hung my coat in the recess while dumping my bag in my desk drawer. I needed another coffee, so I headed off to the staff kitchen to make one. I thought I heard someone come in, but the sound faded away as I waited for the kettle to boil. I spooned in some coffee and added a little milk waiting, god it was taking so long on the first boil. I tapped my fingernails on the countertop, waiting. I heard the door open behind me as arms enveloped me with lips kissing my neck; I knew it was Gus; I turned around to suck him in.

'Mm, I'm glad I came in early,' I said moaning as he started to slide his magic fingers inside of my undies and pulled my blouse to one side of my neck kissing me slowly making me moan in pleasure as I came.

‘Gus we’re going to get caught,’ I said, bringing down my breathing.

It was scary, but it was fun at the same time, like two teenagers, doing stuff in the school closet.

Chapter Fourteen:

'Oh, don't worry about the boss. We are good buddies,' said Gus flexing his eyebrows.

'Really? So, you do him favors, do you?' I said jesting as I slip down to unzip him feeling his hardness, I took his length sucking hard, knowing he would come straight away, which he did. Taking his hot, salty liquid into my mouth, I swallowed, after which I licked him dry and zipped him up. I turned around to continue making my coffee but was overwhelmed as he pulled my blouse to unhook my bra, my breasts falling into his hands. He rolled my nipples between his finger and thumb and bit my neck; I shivered as the sensation kicked in.

'Gus, someone will come in; you're killing me,' I said as I tried to re-dress myself.

‘That’s for not seeing you tonight,’ said Gus, winking as he made his way out of the staff kitchen.

Fuck I was in a fluster; he was starting to get to me. I needed to be with him, and I had made my mind up to take the plunge and move in with him.

I eventually took my coffee back to my desk, now that I had had my pleasure for today, and would miss him tonight, but he was coming down to London Saturday, and I was sure we would make up for the lost time. Matt was the first to ask me if I had applied.

‘No, not yet; the closing date is next week,’ I said, and started reading my emails.

‘Liz, the job is yours; just do it,’ said Matt insisting I applied soon. The staff started coming in as Matt walked off to his office, saying what he wanted to say. The day flew by with the phones ringing non-stop, by 5 pm I was out of the door with the rest of my colleagues now having a train to catch. I didn't have a chance to pack with working last night and being with Gus. I wasn't sure what to pack, not knowing if Emma had any plans for the weekend. I changed in jeans and a black polo neck sweater with a pair of trainers mainly for comfort being a long journey by train. Gus was coming down, so I packed a nice outfit with heels, a couple of tops and underwear, a good job I had my suitcase on wheels.

By the time I texted Emma after reaching London, it was after 10 pm; she met me off the train. There were squeals and hugs as we met.

'Emma, you look fantastic,' I said, hugging her again.

'Look, you don't look bad yourself,' said Emma looking me in the eye, seeing that I had a glint in my eyes. I was looking really happy, despite the wobbly conversation I had with her a few weeks ago.

Emma had a plush apartment in the middle of the city, 'God, Emma, you've landed on your feet with your job.' I said, looking at the décor as we walked into her apartment, it was like a five-star hotel with all the mod cons and gadgets.

'So, where is Lee?' I asked, looking to see if he was around.

'He is out with the lads tonight. I won't see him until tomorrow; he is staying with a colleague from work,' said Emma shrugging the conversation off. Emma showed me to my room. Wow, 6ft four-poster bed! My mind wandered to Gus and having him tied to the bed, pleasuring him without him touching me. Emma went off into the kitchen to make coffee when I came through into the living room; the view from the apartment was amazing, overlooking the city and the quays.

'So, come on, Liz, it's been weeks since you rang me wanting to talk. Spill.' Emma turned slightly to ask me.

I started to tell her what had been happening since she had moved to London, from the time I had gone on holiday and fell for a guy with the pleasures he showed me, the four guys Lottie endured with the help of a fix and posing on stage loving every minute of it. I mentioned Jamie and the guy in the band knowing him saying there was someone in the pub that does a good blow job, and about Jamie using me thinking he could have me as and when he wanted.

I finally started talking about the time I thought I was going to die. Emma gasped, holding her throat as her mouth gaped.

'Oh, Liz, I can't believe you got yourself in that situation.' she hugs me. 'Did you report it to the police?' asked Emma sounding concerned.

‘No, I can’t. I don’t want people to know at work as it will all come out about me, and they will be judging me.’ I said bluntly.

‘But he might do it to someone else,’ said Emma, not letting this go.

‘Look, Emma, I can’t do it, so please stop lecturing me. I thought you would understand.’ I started to weep.

‘Liz, I’m so sorry.’ She hugged me. Changing the subject, Emma chatted about her job and the colleague she worked with. ‘Tomorrow night we will be going to a party, Natasha is always throwing them; is ever so nice and so is her husband. We work together and take it in turns travelling and meeting clients.’

‘Oh, there something else I need to tell you, Emma, I have met someone, and he is coming down tomorrow. I hope you don’t mind.’ I said, sounding nervous, seeing that I was desperate to come down a few weeks ago.

'Liz, I'm pleased for you. Do I know him?' She asked.

'Well, I don't know if I mentioned someone from work to you. I did say I wouldn't get involved again, but with things happening, he was there for me, plus he is gorgeous, and I know I have only seen him a few times, but I think I'm falling for him, Emma.'

'Just be careful and don't get hurt,' said Emma stroking my arm.

'Is it ok, Emma, for him to stay here, or can we get a hotel or something?'

'No, don't be daffed,' said Emma. 'We can all go out to the party tomorrow, can't we?' said Emma.

'Thanks.' I smiled broadly at her.

It was the early hours of the morning before we went to bed, having a catch up on all the gossip, and it wasn't until gone 9 am before I was up. Emma was already up being used to working all hours of the day and night with very little sleep. I padded through into the kitchen in my oversized long tee shirt smelling ground coffee.

'Hmm, that smells nice, makes a change from granulated,' I said as I sniffed the air.

'Hi, did you sleep, ok?' asked Emma pouring a mug for me.

'Yeah that bed is so comfy, you just sink into it,' I said, hugging myself.

'Yeah, want time, will Gus be here?' asked Emma as she passed me the mug.

'He said it depends on the traffic, but it should be about 1 pm; apparently, he has to finish off at work.'

'He works Saturdays? I thought you said he worked in finance,' said Emma, surprised.

'Yes, he does, but he has to get some fingers ready for the board meeting on Monday, that's why he didn't come down with me last night,' I said, trying to justify his excuse. Emma made no comment. 'What time does the party start?' I asked, turning the conversation to the party tonight.

Lee turned up around 1 pm, slamming the door behind him. Emma ignored him and carried on chatting. Was I missing something there?

'Emma, are you and Lee ok?' I asked, fishing for an answer.

'Well sort of,' said Emma sounding unsure.

'Do you want to talk about it?' I asked, sounding her out.

'Well, it started when I moved down here, I was away and came home early, finding him in bed with one of the office girls from his work. I know we are only fuck buddies, but it hurt seeing them together. Then, I did the same to him, making him find me in bed with someone, and he played hell about it. So, we have agreed not to bring partners back to the apartment.' said Emma as she took a nail filer and started to file her nails. I was gobsmacked,

'Emma, I couldn't do what you do; I need stability in my life.'

'Well, that's my life, and it goes with the job,' said Emma as she finished filing her nails.

I was getting worried as it was after 3 pm Gus hadn't turned up. I texted him but had no response. Lee had been in the bathroom showering and was now roaming around after coming out in a towel around his fit, muscular body, flashing his tattoos and body piercings. It was the first time I had seen Lee nearly in the buff, knowing that he had a piercing on the end of his length I bet that felt good.

Emma noticed my eyes watching his body as he walked through to the bedroom.

'Do you want to shag him?' she asked, smirking at me.

I turned in horror in what she had just said. 'Emma, stop it. I have Gus, and I care for him.' I sounded slightly upset that she would say a thing like that.

'Oh, I'm just teasing you.' she jested.

'It's not funny,' I said as I pulled out my phone and tried ringing Gus. It was a while before he answered the phone.

'Sorry, sweetie, I've had a puncture, and the traffic is heavy, but I should be with you in about an hour.'

'God, Gus, I was so worried I thought something might have happened to you,' I said with relief in my voice. Emma had disappeared into the bedroom as I was on the phone with Gus. I could hear laughter and squeals with the sounds moaning of being pleasured. God, how could she be so carefree knowing that he would have probably have been with someone last night and share his bed the following day? I cringed with the thought; I couldn't share Gus with anyone.

I felt slightly lost as Lee pleasured Emma; I made myself another coffee taking it over and stared out across the city and the quays. It was a similar view that Gus had in Manchester. Thinking more about Gus, I didn't know much about him, only a small part of what he had told me. About his job in finance and his unruly mess of blond hair, how did he get away with it? All the managers I had seen either had short-cropped hair or with some style, Gus was neither. Why was Gus the only one having to deal with the financial figures for the board meeting on Monday?

The doorbell rang; I jumped in surprise, being in a world of my own. I ran to open the door; there stood Gus still looking cool despite the long and troublesome journey down. I jumped, wrapping my legs around his waist, smothering him with kisses; I needed him inside me. I jumped down as he picked up his overnight case walking in looking at the décor of the apartment.

'Emma's got a nice apartment,' said Gus as I closed the door behind him.

'Yes, it is nice; the view is similar to yours,' I said.

'Yes, where am I sleeping tonight?' said Gus smirking at me.

'Well, loverboy, we have a nice comfy bed with extras,' I said, winking at him.

'You better show me, then sweetie.' He sounded sexy. We were in the bedroom fast; his brows rose after seeing the four-poster bed. I had his trousers down; his length was waiting for my mouth as I pushed him onto the bed and took him hard to give him instant relief of pleasure and swallowing all his hot salty liquid before coming up to kiss him passionately on his lips. We savoured the moment exchanging tongues, with a sudden movement, he was on top of me his strength overpowering me as we started to play fight to the point, we both finished naked on the bed. I was calling his name as he found all my sensitive areas using them to the max, making me come over and over again. We were panting and sweaty with our work out but enjoyed every minute of it.

Emma was still in the bedroom with Lee as we both padded off to the bathroom to have more pleasure and wash our bodies of sweat and bodily fluids. Once we had finished, we padded back to the bedroom, wrapped in a towel. Emma and Lee were seated on the sofa drinking coffee; both dressed in lightweight robes after their time of intimacy.

'Hi Gus,' shouted Emma as we walked across to the bedroom.

'Hi Emma and Lee,' said Gus looking a little out of his depth.

'I am making a fresh pot of coffee. Would you both like one?' asked Lee, jumping up, heading for the kitchen.

'Yes, please, as we both said it in unison.'

The conversation was slightly tense, but eventually, it became easy as Emma brought out the wine. The party started at 8 pm, and we had to drink water to compensate for drinking too much before the party had started. We started to get ready for the party, but were preoccupied with having more pleasures in the bedroom; our moans could be heard as Emma and Lee were in the bathroom. Gus wore a pair of brown chinos with a cream shirt and brown shoes. He looked handsome as the colour brought out his piercing blue eyes and unruly blond messy hair. I applied my make-up before putting my outfit.

Gus caught me unaware, sliding his hand inside my lacy undies while he unhooked my lacy bra letting my breasts fall, cupping one as he worked his magic fingers below and his finger and thumb on my hard nipple as he started to pull. Pushing my head back, I moaned with pleasure as he kissed my neck, making me come quickly. He pushed me on the bed, sliding off my undies, parting my legs to drink my wetness as he pulled my nipples, sending a sensation, giving me another orgasm.

I lay thereafter he had finished, I could stay in this room all night making love to him instead of going to the party.

'Gus?' I said.

'Hmm, what's up, my sweet?' said Gus standing over me with his length hard beneath his trousers.

'Gus fuck me hard,' I said, raising my brow and licking my lips, within seconds, he was inside me pumping hard. My breasts wobbled as he pumped me, and within seconds, his pleasure came. At least he had his release before going to the party.

By the time we were ready and dressed for the party, it was late, and it was after 8 pm when we arrived. The apartment block was one of the most expensive areas in London. As we entered the building, there was a plush reception area; I was gobsmacked to see how the other half lived. I marveled at the type of colleagues Emma worked with, showing that they had money. Would I fit in only working in sales, taking orders, and selling clearance stocks?

We soon arrived at the apartment; the door was slightly ajar for the arrivals to excess the apartment without having to knock. Emma pushed the door open; we could hear music playing in the background. The apartment was huge, with half being open plan for the living area overlooking the centre of London. The floors were laid with solid wood with services in stainless steel, making the apartment looking a little clinical.

There were several people already there as they milled around to talk pleasantries. I needed the bathroom in which Emma pointed me in the right direction while the rest of them went to meet their hosts. The bathroom was huge, as with everything inside it. I ran my fingers along the sides of the walls feeling the textures. I must have been in at least 5 minutes, but as I came out, I couldn't see Gus amongst the guests. I pushed my way through smiling, searching for Gus, and then someone grabbed me by the arm, I turned, expecting to find Gus, but no it was Luke.

'Hello Liz, it's a surprise to see you here,' said Luke kissing me on the lips.

I stood there frozen, not knowing what to say; Luke was the last person I would ever expect to see again.

‘Hi, Luke,’ I said, remembering the last time I was with him showing me different ways of pleasuring and how I fell for him. But now I had Gus giving me my pleasures. I was slowly starting to fall in love with him.

‘So, who have you come with?’ asked Luke, sounding me out.

‘Erm, I’ve come with Emma and my boyfriend,’ I said, trying to draw a line between us.

‘Oh, I’ll introduce you to my wife,’ said Luke sounding normal as though I had not been with him. He kept hold of my wrist, towing me through the crowd to find his wife.

As Luke opened the door to the kitchen, there stood Gus with his wife Natasha with their arms around each other, my face dropped seeing them together. They pulled apart as we walked in, it seemed that Natasha had been crying. Gus looked up, looking at my face, shocked with his betrayal until he saw Luke holding my wrist. That was when the argument started. The penny had dropped with me meeting Luke on holiday and telling Gus briefly about my feelings. Gus was nearly married, and that was to Natasha, but she chose Luke. Luke and Gus had been to university studying finance and were best buddies until Natasha went off with Luke.

'You took my ex, and now you have my girlfriend, you bastard?' Gus went over and took a swing at Luke. I couldn't believe this was happening, it was a chance in a million that I would ever see Luke again, and it had happened. It was all too much, so I ran out trying to find Emma. I could see her sitting near the window, rushing across. I asked for the keys to the apartment I had to go to.

'What's wrong, Liz?' she asked in surprise.

'It's Luke and Gus they know each other and Natasha left Gus for Luke, just give me the key, I've got to get out of here,' I said, my eyes were welling up, ready to burst. Emma handed me the key, and I disappeared fast out of the apartment. I needed to process this; it was turning out all wrong, with male pride getting in the way.

I arrived at Emma's apartment, tears streaming down my face. I undressed and changed into my jeans and top; needed to go home, I couldn't stay. So I packed my things within 10 minutes I was out of the door leaving the key in the mailbox downstairs. I texted Emma at the station, but she didn't reply, probably too much to drink. I was lucky it was the last one running back to Manchester that night. My thoughts on the train wandered back to Gus, why did I have to get involved with someone from work? And what were the odds of him meeting his ex with Luke been married to her? I was jinxed.

I could now understand why he reacted like that having a double whammy firstly his best mate taking his ex and now had pleasures with his girlfriend, snatching both from him. This was male pride coming out, why couldn't he let it go? I told Gus my problems with the guys I was with and about meeting Luke, but he didn't question it, he still wanted to see me.

By the time I got home, it was nearly 1.30 am the flat was in darkness as I opened the door. I was tired from the journey crying, knowing everything was fucked up in my life again. I heard a noise thinking it must be either Lottie or Alice, but as I opened my bedroom door, switching the lights on there stood in the middle of my room was a guy dressed in black. My heart dropped in the pits of my stomach; it was Al the grim reaper who had a personality transplant and throttled me.

I ran to the door in a panic knowing what could happen if he caught me, but he ruby tackled me down to the floor, hitting my head on the corner of the small cupboard stood in the hallway of the door. The pain shot through my head as I blacked out.

As I came around, my head pounded, and I wondered where I was. I was back in my bedroom lying on my bed, expecting to be tied and naked, but I wasn't. Relief surged through me, knowing at least I had a chance to fight. I started to sit up, assessing if he was still here. I quince as I propped myself up to go to get some pain killers for my head. But there he was, sat watching me from the chair near the door. I flopped back onto the bed, fuck I didn't have the energy to fight. He came over and stroked my face with the back of his hand, not saying a word.

I stiffened as he touched me, not knowing what he was going to do, his hand traced over my lips, running his finger along the line. He brought his head down, grazing his lips on mine gently. I didn't react; I was terrified as he could change anytime, forcing me to be in the same situation I was in before. My breathing was starting to get heavy, which he could see as my chest could be seen stressing with his presence but did not comment. He kissed my forehead, where I had hit my head as I quince in pain as I waited, thinking about how I could get out of this before his personality changed. I should have stayed in London; I seemed to make all the bad choices was this going to be the end? The silence was killing me; why didn't he say something at least I would know what mood he was in? I needed to get some pain killers, so I moved, thinking at least this would give me some idea of his intentions.

Al stopped standing up, giving me room to move, my head pounding as I got up from the bed; he was watching me with no expression on his face. I walked to the door, where he followed me into the kitchen as I found the tablets for my head. He shadowed me to the bathroom, but I wanted to shut him out while I peed, but he was by my side, waiting. I plodded back to my bedroom, knowing I couldn't escape. He had been with me for over an hour in silence; the suspense was killing me, so I went for it.

‘Al, what do you want from me?’ I asked, sounding desperate for him to speak to me. There was a pause.

‘I’m putting you through a test,’ he said in a normal voice.

‘Test, what test?’ I asked, thinking, what the fuck was this about?

‘You didn’t go to the police when I nearly strangled you,’ he said as his fingers rubbed across my lips.

‘No,’ I whispered, avoiding eye contact with him.

‘But we know why, don’t we, Liz? He lifted my chin, looking into my eyes.

‘I suppose so,’ I whispered.

‘Tell me, Liz.’ he squeezed my face making my lips go into an o shape. ‘Liz, tell Al the reasons.’ He squeezed tighter, I grabbed his hand and tried to pull him away, but I had pushed him too far for he pushed me down on the bed with his hand now around my neck squeezing tightly. My hands hanging on his trying to get some relief, I started to struggle flailing my body trying to escape, but the weight of his body on top of me held me firm. He kissed me as he held me by the throat. He was fucking with me being nice one minute and nearly killing me the next, was this his way of jerking off?

He kept on kissing me and throttling me, I had stopped struggling and had no fight in me, my head was aching despite taking the pain killers, and my love life was in tatters, so I gave up the fight, it was in his hands whether I lived or died, I just didn't care anymore. He stopped eventually, getting up from my bed, I lay there not know what he was going to do next. I closed my eyes, wanting him to go, but went I opened them; he had his length waiting for some attention. Oh fuck, this wasn't going to happen to me again. He lifted me as my mouth faced his length; he didn't say anything at first as he pushed his length in my face acknowledging me to take it in my mouth. I ignored him as he pushed further.

I kept my mouth firmly shut. He became agitated by my refusal and took hold of my hair, pulling me back.

'You slag, open your mouth,' my head was banging as he held my hair tightly, forcing me to suck him. I refused, despite the pain from my head. He kept on calling me slag as I still refused, his temper was now showing in his eyes, but I didn't care. He let go of my hair, and suddenly, without notice, he punched me in the face causing my lip to bleed as I fell flat on my bed. He tucked in his length and started using me as a punching bag as the blood-spattered the walls. I was trying to stop the blows, but he was holding me with one hand and using his other on my face as my lips started to swell with blood pouring from my cuts.

'Was I going to die being a punching bag for him?' He stopped after he had punched about four times, as his eyes softened, he picked me up, wrapping his arms around me, kissing my pounded lips gently. I lifted my hand feeling his face as I couldn't see very well as my eye were moist with tears while swelling up. I felt his hair and held on to it as he jerked back; I scratched his face, his mood changed again, and his last punch came down hard on my face, and with that, I had blacked out.

I woke up not knowing where I was, but I could hear voices around me. I was in the hospital, my face so swollen I couldn't see out of my eyes, my face was like a balloon, and my lip was that swollen I could only drink from a straw.

'Liz, it's me, Lottie.' I felt someone squeeze my hand. I groaned to acknowledge her as I couldn't speak. 'Liz, I thought you were dead when I came in and saw all that blood on the walls,' said Lottie rubbing my hand. I groaned. Lottie stayed for half an hour before leaving. I didn't know what time of day or even what day it was. I was thinking of Gus; I shouldn't run out on him like that, if I hadn't, then probably this wouldn't have happened. I was now at my lowest point. Had I lost the perfect man in my life?

I had lost track of time being in the hospital, only Lottie visiting me every other day only to say hello and staying for 10 minutes. The police wanted to speak to me now I could talk. My life couldn't get any worse with the police asking me questions about my ordeal and if I knew who my attacker was. What had I to lose Gus hadn't come to see me was this a sign telling me it was over? I told the police everything, including the attack before. Swabs had been taken from my clothes and fingernails as I tried to describe Al to the police.

It was over a month before I could go back to work; my face still had bruising from my ordeal. The police had caught Al he had preyed on someone else being disturbed and was caught in the act. I was nervous about going back to work as my colleagues would be asking me questions about it. I didn't want to talk about it; it was too raw having to go to court and submit my statement in a courtroom.

The first day had arrived to go back to work. I was in for 8.30 am as my colleagues welcomed me back into the office but didn't ask me questions about my ordeal, knowing I was due to give evidence in court. Matt, the Sales Manager, had left starting a new position in another branch. I didn't have the opportunity to apply for his job with it being late while I was in the hospital missing the deadline. I should have done it as soon as Anne had said and not left it until the last minute. Jim had been offered the job of Sales Manager; he came out and gave me a hug welcoming me back. I couldn't be any lower than I was now. It was looking as though I needed to find a new job once again as I sat at my desk, trolling through hundreds of emails over the last month. My heart wasn't in it anymore as I had not seen Gus since that night in London.

The calls were taken by my colleagues while I answered my emails until I had a call from Janet, who was the PR for the CEO of the company.

'Hello, Liz, I hope you are feeling better now. We all have missed you so much,' said Janet sounding sincere.

'Oh, thanks, Janet,' I said, depressed.

'Liz, CEO Alfie Patterson, wants to see you when you're ready. He has no meetings today, so when you're ready,' said Janet sounding upbeat now.

'What does he want to see me for?' I asked, surprised as I had never seen him before and so had many others.

'I don't know he just asked me if you would go and see him,' said Janet sounding as though she had no clues what it was about. I put the receiver down, turning to Anne, who had been listening in on my call.

'Why does the CEO Alfie Patterson, want to see me?' I asked Anne in shock.

'Oh, you'll have to let me know,' said Anne needing gossip.

In between two coffees and finishing my emails, which took me an hour and a half, I decided to make my way to the CEO's office. Of course, it had to be right at the top of the building, so I was relieved that there was a lift to take me up to the top floor. I was thinking about Gus wondering what floor he was on as I waited for the lift to stop. As soon as the lift stopped, I straightened my skirt, pushing my hair back over my shoulders before stepping out from the lift. I stepped out in a long corridor with more offices having glass sides seeing the remainder of the top management working in their offices. Janet's office was part of the open plan of the corridor with the CEO's office the full size of the side end of the building, which overlooked the city.

Janet was petite, having blond hair, being in her late fifties; she was on the phone when I arrived. She pointed to the door indicating for me to go straight in. I felt nervous as I knocked on the door, I didn't hear my acknowledgement, so I knocked louder. I heard someone shout come in, I opened the door and walked in not knowing what to expect until I saw Gus sat at a large dark oak desk talking on the phone as he waved me in.

I stood there looking around to see where Alfie Patterson was, is this some sick joke? I thought as I closed the door behind me. Gus quickly ended the call as he stood up, walking over to envelop me in his arms, I froze. He kissed me softly on the lips, whispering sorry.

I was finding it hard to process all this, where was Alfie Patterson?

'Liz, I am so sorry I didn't come to see you earlier; my mother was dying, and things had to be sorted.' He hugged me tightly, kissing the top of my head. I was still waiting for Alfie Patterson to come in. Gus pressed the intercom, Janet, can you bring us some coffees.

'Yes, Mr. Patterson,' said Janet.

'Are you Alfie Patterson?' I stared at Gus in disbelief.

He looked at me with those piercing blue eyes and unruly messy hair; this was how he got away with his hair, he owned the company, he had deceived me saying he worked in finance, was I that gullible?

Janet knocked on the door before she came in with the tray of coffee and biscuits. Gus still had his arm around me, but Janet just grinned as she put the tray on the desk.

'Thanks, Janet,' said Gus.

'Is there anything else you need?' asked Janet before she left.

'No, but don't put any calls through to me until I say,' said Gus.

'Sure, Mr. Patterson.' She left the room, grinning from ear to ear. So it was true, Gus was Alfie Patterson. I was still processing all this. I thought my life was over walking away from a situation I couldn't handle and nearly getting killed by a mad man in the process.

'Gus, why didn't you tell me who you were from the start?' I said, looking into his piercing blue eyes for answers.

'Because you wouldn't have opened up as you did and not be your normal self, would you, Liz?' said Gus hugging me as he kissed gently on the lips. 'When I saw Natasha at the party, we were both in shock, knowing she had made a mistake; I was comforting her telling her I had met the love of my life in you. Despite the fact, you had been with my best friend Luke, from university who also had taken Natasha from me ten years ago. Natasha had made her choice with Luke, and it didn't work out. I had to swallow my pride knowing Luke was the guy who showed you different types of pleasure only I wished it had been me, but I am willing to live with that.' said Gus as he kissed me passionately on the lips.

His taste and touch waking my body from having endured pain of waiting to be loved once more.

'Oh, Gus, I am so sorry I ran I couldn't handle it seeing you with someone else. I am starting to fall in love with you.' I sobbed as I returned his kiss with more passion.

'But I have, Liz, the day I first saw you in the staff kitchen trying to get away from your embarrassment,' said

Gus grinning at me. Our coffee went cold, but none of us cared.

'So, where do we go from here?' I said, knowing he had blown his cover.

'Well, for a start, you are moving out of the flat and quitting that bar job you have, I don't want guys ogling at you, but you could dress up for me if you like,' said Gus giving me a raised brow.

'Hmm. That sounds good to me, especially the dressing up bit.' I giggled as I went down and took his length in my mouth and sucked him hard.

About the Author:

Sue Vout, currently living a peaceful secluded life in a village near Gainsborough, Lincolnshire, England started writing as a student but is now a full-time writer. Her love for nature and animals turned her sensitive and nudged her to share her thoughts through her stories. Finding joy in short walks, music, art and nature, Sue has always loved the idea of spreading joy and beauty of the world through her writing. Her philosophy of life is reaching the stars while you still can, as waiting for the right moment is stupid. Every moment is the right moment if you see it closely. In her world, women are strong, brave and are capable of living life as they want, true love still exists, and chivalry is not dead.

Made in the USA
Coppell, TX
02 June 2021